THE LONG WALK HOME

By the same author:

The Devil's Prison
Doctor! Doctor!

THE LONG WALK HOME

by

MICHAEL O'DONNELL

LONDON
VICTOR GOLLANCZ LTD
1988

First published in Great Britain 1988
by Victor Gollancz Ltd
14 Henrietta Street, London WC2E 8QJ

British Library Cataloguing in Publication Data
O'Donnell, Michael, *1928–*
 The long walk home.
 I. Title
 823'.914[F]   PR6065.D/

ISBN 0-575-04196-X

Set in Great Britain by Centracet
and printed in Great Britain by
St Edmundsbury Press Ltd, Bury St Edmunds, Suffolk

For Shirley and Glyn Houston,
Anne and Bob Kellett,
Angela and Francis Matthews,
— and, of course, Catherine.

Chapter One

Two hundred and seventy-four . . . two hundred and seventy-five . . .

He watched each drop as it swelled at the point of a leaf eight inches from his forehead then tried to count it at the very instant it detached itself to splash on to the leaf below. Two hundred and seventy-six . . .

A bit like counting sheep. Maybe it would prove as soporific. Better stop. He couldn't afford to fall asleep now. He blessed the rain. Heavy enough to deter the grockles—gawping tourists—but not the enthusiasts. He hadn't blessed it in the night when he'd stumbled through the dark, not daring to use a torch, and trying to pick his way along the dried-out bed of the Manifold River. He'd made the woods below Rushley with little time to spare, just as the sky started to lighten.

Five days before he'd been a respectable person who wore a suit to work but now he'd become a creature of the night. When the sun was up he slept under bushes, heated cans of soup on his tiny calor stove, or stared at the sky and brooded; when the sun went down he emerged to scramble along half-seen paths, trip over unseen rocks, tear his skin on brambles.

Tonight all that would change. Tonight, Bill Marsden, you will sleep in a bed with real sheets and real pillows. But tonight will come only if you stay alert.

Two hundred and seventy-eight . . . two hundred and seventy-nine . . .

This morning, when he skirted Ilam Hall under a lightening sky, and passed the bubble holes through which the river re-emerged from its underground course, back had come the sound that had accompanied every remembered walk of childhood and adolescence, water chuckling across stones. As Bill grew aware of it, he'd stepped out, shoulders back, rucksack steady between his shoulder-blades, stick carried at the trail—

7

he couldn't afford the tap tap of the ferrule on the pathway—
as though setting out for a day's walking through the White
Peaks.

That had been two hours before yet he still retained the
confidence the brisk walk had engendered. He'd repacked his
tiny stove in his rucksack and now sat on a pile of leaves, his
stomach lined with yet another canful of tomato soup, within a
familiar shelter of childhood: the cave, the wigwam, the igloo—
depended on which game you were playing—formed by the
arched branches of a rhododendron. Its branches screened him
from the path below and he focused his attention on the lawn
at the other side of the river beyond the narrow stone bridge.

He wished those bloody ramblers would start their day.
Maybe the youth hostellers had given up Ilam Hall. He'd been
sitting here for two hours and had seen not a shadow of human
presence around the quaint old chunk of nineteenth-century
baronial. Two hundred and ninety . . . two hundred and ninety-
one . . .

Then suddenly they were there. Socks red, socks blue, socks
grey, boots brown, anoraks dark green, bright blue, orange, or
red; a flock of ramblers drifting, acknowledging, regrouping on
the lawn. He pulled the hood of his own anorak over his head,
slipped his arms through the harness of his rucksack and
slithered down the slope of the path. He strolled with overcal-
culated nonchalance across the bridge and hovered on the
outskirts of the pack, nodding a smiling "Hello" at any face
that turned his way. He was rewarded with friendly and
unsuspicious "Hello"s in return.

A few stragglers still came from the house and he assessed
the groupings forming on the lawn. He wanted to find two
people walking together. A larger group might prove too
difficult to handle. Too many questions coming from too many
people and demanding consistent evasion. Yet he didn't want
to walk on his own. A solitary walker would invite suspicion; a
group of three wouldn't merit a second glance. It was nearly
two days since he last saw a patrol but he could never assume
that he was winning. And this was the day he was forced to
take the biggest risk. He spotted the couple he needed. A man
and a woman, older than the others, stood together, con-

sciously detached from the rest of the pack. The man had a neat grey beard, was roughly Bill's height, which would make him six foot oneish. but maybe ten years younger, which would make him forty-twoish. His companion was also tall, dark hair bundled under anorak hood, mid-twenties, and attractive in a buxom sort of way. Middle-aged ramblers seemed to have a happy knack for finding wholesome walking companions.

As the pack moved off down the drive Bill extended his stride until he was alongside the couple he'd decided to latch on to.

"Did you catch the forecast?" he asked.

"Said it should lighten later this morning then piss down again after mid-day. Though I often wonder whether the buggers ever really know what they're talking about."

The man's accent was West Riding. The woman said nothing. Just smiled and nodded.

The pack processed from the drive across the village square and queued at the stile that led to the lower slopes of Bunster Hill.

"It's a tight schedule today," said the man.

Bill took his cue from the girl and just smiled.

There was little chatter from the walkers. They strode along in groups of twos and threes, walking not talking. And he was among them. Camouflaged. His pursuers were looking for an individual and he was submerged in a group. For the first time since he left the Centre he was walking across open country in daylight, or what served for daylight on a dull September day, thanks to a disguise he had found in a memory of a childhood picnic. If he'd had one more day, he could have traversed this last stretch, as he'd traversed every other stretch, by night. But he didn't have another day. If he didn't make the rendezvous by six this evening, the game was lost.

The walkers descended the slope towards the entrance to Dovedale. Below them the tourist car park was all but empty. In one corner, a green and white trailer proclaimed its purpose in large letters on its side: "Peak National Park Information Service". Alongside it stood another trailer which, if unshuttered, might serve food and drink. Just the sight of it made Bill salivate like a Pavlovian dog: the afternoon before he had dreamed of fish and chips. In the furthest corner stood the solitary car that seems as much part of a deserted car park as the solitary suitcase on the luggage carousel of a deserted airport.

As they queued at the double stile above the car park, the bearded man raised his hand and pointed at the top of Thorpe Cloud. From where they stood the towering hill looked as though it had a flat top, a miniature table mountain, and on the table, silhouetted against grey cloud, stood three figures.

"They've got up there early," he said.

Bill tugged instinctively at the forelock of his hood and concentrated his attention on his boots. He'd taken one swift glance at the silhouettes. They were too far away to see any detail. And, to them the walkers would be just animated shapes, but Bill was willing to bet that all three had field-glasses held to their eyes.

He felt hopelessly exposed, standing there in the queue like a microbe fixed to a slide and lined up for magnified scrutiny. To feel secure, he had to keep moving. He caught himself edging forward impatiently and drew an angry "Watch it" from the man he pushed against. He mumbled an apology and drifted back to the dark girl and the bearded man. He needed urgently to be a member of a threesome.

"Been through Dovedale before?" he asked.

"At least twice a year since I were a kid."

"Ron's a great walker," said the girl.

They reached the stiles, clambered over, and followed the procession along the metalled road that led into Dovedale gorge.

"People don't think about the construction of a walk these days," said Ron. "Only interested in bloody mileage. That's television for you. Everything has to be competitive. They don't use maps no more, just *The Guinness Book of Records*. A walk should have harmony and construction. Like a symphony. An energetic climb, a pastoral interlude, mebbe at a summit, a cheeky downhill scherzo, and a rewarding journey home along the flat."

Bill seemed to listen as attentively as did the dark-haired woman. He bent his head—and his hood—close to Ron's as if fearful of missing a syllable. But it wasn't the words that had caught his attention.

As they'd rounded the bend beyond the car park, he'd seen a police car parked on the cattle grid that filled the only gap in the fence that stretched across the dale. The walkers would have to filter between the ends of the fence and the sides of the car. And, as they did, each would pass within a foot or two of the alert policemen who sat in the front seats.

Bill's hand moved instinctively to his chin to stroke the beard he no longer possessed. His new clean-shavenness was a pretty thin disguise. The first thing they would have done was paint out the beard on his photograph. The men in the car would have two pictures of the elusive Dr Marsden, one with and one without. And then, miraculously, ten yards from the police car, the leaders of the pack turned right towards a footbridge that crossed the river. Bill contrived to stay on the side of the bunch furthest from the car.

Once they were across the bridge and beneath the steep slope of Thorpe Cloud, the leaders of the pack quickened their stride and Ron's lungs grew too busy to push out words. Bill didn't mind. The only creatures to have them under observation now were the few sheep whose search for the elusive greener grass had led them to the top of the hills that flanked the entrance to the gorge. Bill enjoyed the walking. An hour before, each limb had felt so stiff and bruised he feared he could coax few more miles from them. But now, as he matched the rhythm set by those ahead, his legs moved easily and the stick in his right hand measured out the pace with the jaunty precision of an RSM trying to enthuse a bunch of recruits. And, as the regular rhythm of his muscles came more and more under automatic control, so his spirits began to rise.

He'd once read that joggers become addicted to their exercise because their muscles push something into their bloodstream that affects their cerebral cortex and makes them feel "high". Maybe walking had the same effect. Or did the rhythmical beat of foot on ground produce regular electrical impulses that travelled along the sensory nerves and helped clear the cerebral computer? This was no time for physiology. He was on the last lap home and he had survived.

•

They passed the stepping-stones that spanned the Dove and, as they crossed the last stretch of riverside grass, a patch of sunlight appeared high on the other side of the gorge as if the sun were trying to spotlight the odd rocky edifice that emerged from the trees and was known to some as Dovedale Church, to others as Dovedale Castle.

The walkers were now strung out like cyclists in a road race, even more so as they climbed the narrow steps towards Sharplow Point. Bill made use of the excuse to fall behind Ron and his lady.

He carried a childhood memory of Sharplow, the grey rock that overhung the river and was known inevitably as Lover's Leap. His father had lowered himself from the top of the rock till his feet rested on a ridge on the far side and then had teased his mother that he couldn't get back. Bill remembered his mother, terrified but determined not to lose face, half pretending to be worried and half being very worried indeed. She had turned abruptly on her son and ordered him shrilly to keep away from the edge and not to be stupid like his father.

When they reached the top of the climb, there was the rock exactly as he had remembered it. He left the others, climbed out on to the ledge that overhung the river, closed his eyes and sought to conjure up that jovial, slightly eccentric person who had been his father.

A gruff voice sounded in his ear. "Don't do anything stupid, now. You're supposed to find the lover first and leap later."

Ron had climbed on to the rock behind him and his lady stood where Bill's mother had once stood.

Ron bent, picked up an empty cigarette package, and stuffed it into a side pocket of his rucksack.

"Bloody vandals," he said. "If I'd seen the yobbo who dropped that I'd have had him over the side before he'd had time to read the government health warning."

The path from the rock ran downhill and made no demands on Ron's oxygen supply. He droned on like a tour guide, pointing out each group of rocky needles or buttresses that rose from the trees on the far side of the gorge. They all had a name, allegedly descriptive, but only for those possessed of an energetic imagination: Twelve Apostles, Jacob's Ladder,

Church Rocks. Ron had a story to go with each, sometimes local legend, more often an account of what had happened to him or a friend when once they walked this way.

At Reynard's Cave he told the tale of an eighteenth-century Irish dean visiting Derby who had come there on a picnic. After the meal, the dean mounted his horse, invited a young woman to climb up behind him, and tried to ride up the side of the gorge. The horse slipped and the dean was killed. On the Sunday before, he had preached at All Saints', Derby, and chosen as his text: "You know not the day nor the hour."

"What happened to the young woman?" asked Ron's dark-haired lady.

"Dunno," said Ron.

But the question had discomforted him. Maybe because of its source. He shook his head in puzzlement, turned away from them both and said no more.

That suited Bill. Ron had served his purpose and was now turning from asset to hazard because Bill needed to detach himself from the pack before they reached the end of the gorge. He lagged a few paces behind Ron and the woman.

The gorge now narrowed till there was room only for river and path between the walls of rock that rose from the river bed and, as the path entered the straits, it became a duck-board footway. When they reached the footway, Bill stood aside, in what appeared to be a courteous gesture to allow others to pass ahead. Then he knelt on one knee and fiddled with a bootlace until everyone had passed.

The walkers had accelerated again and, within seconds, the tail-enders had disappeared from view. Bill dawdled after them taking his time. He wouldn't put it past Ron to wait for him at the far end of the straits so he paused, leaned on his stick, and watched the water rushing over the stones a yard from his feet.

Two days before, when he'd been trying to catch some sleep wrapped in a sleeping-bag and coiled under a bush in the woods above Fernilee, he had realized that a man passed one of life's milestones when innocent memories of childhood became symbols of mortality. The stones he could see on the river bed, through the clear water, must have been there when he walked by as a child, just as they must have been there when the Iris' dean walked by before his picnic. And two hundred years from now, when all evidence of his existence was long gone, the stones would still be there with water rushing over them. The priests who taught him at school had been deceivers. It was the stones and the river which had found the secret of eternal life.

For a moment, doubt entered his mind. If he could turn the clock back six days, would he re-embark on this bizarre adventure or would he accept what seemed to be inevitable and settle for the real things in life, like respect for authority and index-linked pensions? He might think he was playing the hero but the stones on the river bed remained unmoved. Only tonight would he discover if he had achieved anything at all.

Too late now for doubt. He took his weight off the stick, turned, and walked slowly along the path. He noticed, for the first time, that the sky had cleared and the morning sun was reaching into the gorge. As the straits opened out and he passed beneath the Lion's Head—one rock that *did* live up to its name and uncannily so—he looked apprehensively ahead for signs of a lurking Ron. But the path was clear.

He continued to walk slowly and when he came to Ilam rock, which rose from the floor of the gorge like the barnacled fin of a submarine, he crossed the footbridge beneath it.

At the far side of the river, the main track turned right towards Hall Dale but a narrower path turned left, swept up over some tall rocks and then seemed to peter out amid the scrub that covered the slope. If the memory of his father and himself labouring up that slope had not been so persistent, he would have turned back. Instead he pressed on, stopping often to try and guess where the next bit of identifiable path might lie, occasionally having to haul himself up a short rock face with no confidence that beyond it would be a surface on which to rest or even step.

But this was one childhood memory that did not play him false and on a ridge, some hundred feet above the river, he found what he was looking for, a tall rounded bush with exuberant outer foliage which masked its barren centre; one of the natural shelters that had been his daily resting place since he took to the road. He pulled an outer branch aside, used his stick to clear a few brambles that grew across the leaves

14

covering the ground, unpacked his waterproof sleeping-bag and pushed it into the shelter. He sat on a rock outside.

He was high enough up the slope to be in the sun and it warmed his back as he heated up his last tin of soup. Not by chance, this last one was tomato. He'd hoarded it in much the same way when, as a child, he'd made sure the last wine-gum was a blackcurrant one. Below him he could see the path on the far side of the river, now deserted.

He packed away his mug and stove, pushed his rucksack into the shelter to use as a pillow, crawled in after it and, pulling his sleeping-bag around him, lay coiled upon the ground. His legs were once again stiff and painful but he barely noticed the discomfort. The climb up the slope had wearied him, and the warm soup had made him feel sleepy. He set the alarm on his watch for five-thirty; it would surely take no more than fifteen minutes to reach Milldale. Then he fell into a restless sleep.

He was wakened by the sound of rain tapping on the leaves above him and, when he looked at his watch, he found he had been asleep for only ten minutes. He crawled deeper into his shelter and listened to the beat of raindrops rising in crescendo.

Over the past few weeks he'd grown used to lying still, thinking he was awake yet realizing he was sinking into sleep because the thoughts that spun slowly yet insistently in his mind began to turn from reality to fantasy.

The same process started again. He thought about young Craddock, that lock of fair hair falling across his forehead and the eagerness with which he'd talked of the future on the first morning Bill had arrived at the Centre and Craddock had been detailed to show him round. There was something he wanted to ask Craddock, something to do with his father's atlas and a fox, but his horse was waiting and he leaped into the saddle and Craddock leaped on behind, clasping Bill's waist tightly with both arms. And off they charged at the slope of the gorge.

They jumped the picnic hamper and the cloth that lay beyond it. The most important thing in their lives was that they should reach the top before it was too late yet the slope grew steeper and steeper till they were climbing a vertical wall. Yet still the horse kept galloping, clasping cracks and crevices with prehensile hooves. Craddock shouted in Bill's ear and pointed upwards. They were climbing the inside surface of an arch and, as Bill looked, they were upside down and those magical hooves lost their adhesion and horse and he and Craddock fell back into gloom, falling separately, spinning slowly, down towards an insistent electronic bleep.

He hauled himself awake and switched off the alarm in his watch. He rubbed his eyes, swilled out his mouth with all that was left in his water-bottle—he'd have no further need of that—then crawled from his shelter. The rain had turned to a persistent drizzle. He turned up his hood, slipped his arms through the harness of his rucksack for the last time, and started to scramble down over the rocks and mud. His legs were still stiff and painful and no matter how often he reminded himself that he was on the last lap, his spirit remained as grey as the sky.

Coming down a steep slope is always more difficult than climbing it and he was glad when he reached the footbridge. He crossed it and turned left along the path the walkers had taken nine hours before. He hoped that, now he could stride out, the rhythm of the walk would have its usual therapeutic effect. But this time it failed him. Fatigue and a debt of sleep accumulated over six days seemed finally to have caught up with him. Why now, when he was so near his goal and the path ahead was clear?

He accelerated up the slight slope that led past the caves marking the end of the gorge before it opened out to less rugged pasture. That burst of energy made him feel better but he caught his toe on a stone and the lace on his right boot jumped from its topmost hook.

He had to go down on one knee to retie the lace. It was the luckiest move he had made that day.

As he finished the tying and raised his head he saw, two hundred yards ahead, a line of policemen spread out across the dale and advancing slowly towards him. If he hadn't bent his head and hidden his face beneath his dark-green hood, they would surely have spotted him.

He quickly lowered his head again, turned, and scuttled back along the path, bent double, expecting that at any moment a shout would strike him in the back like a bullet. But no shout came and he was round the corner and out of their sight. If he hurried back to the footbridge and up the slope he had climbed earlier, he might be able to get to Ilam Top and round by the road in time to make the fall-back rendezvous at nine o'clock.

He didn't run but walked briskly, trying to read his map as he moved. What he saw was reassuring. There was a path up the slope to Ilam Top and, if he could find it, he should make the fall-back rendezvous in time. No need to panic. He lengthened his pace and back came the old exhilaration of the walk. His bloodstream washed the pain from his legs; eagerness and a sense of purpose washed the depression from his brain.

He rounded the corner before the footbridge and there, leaning all alone against its rail, was a familiar figure. Ron. What the hell could Bill say that would allow him to get past quickly and up the track on the far side of the river? But, even as he considered the problem, Ron solved it for him.

From fifteen yards away he shouted: "Stay exactly where you are, Dr Marsden. Absolutely still. This gun in my hand is loaded and the safety catch is off. So let's stay here nice and easy until my uniformed friends catch up with us."

The adrenalin pumping round Bill's body swept him into unthinking reaction. He didn't stop but accelerated, lowered his head, and flung himself at his adversary. His head drove hard into Ron's midriff, Ron lost his balance and, as he fell backwards, his head struck a rock with a soft thudding noise.

Bill didn't wait to see what had happened but sprinted across the bridge and headed for the track on the left. He threw off his rucksack, no further need for that, and started to climb. The rain had made the footholds and handholds on the slope more treacherous than he remembered and, as he passed his shelter of the afternoon, he heard shouts in the gorge below. They'd found Ron. They'd be on their radio now, rustling up cover for Ilam Top. Nothing he could do but try to get there before the cover did.

Climbing grew more difficult. The sky was still light, though greyed by cloud, but he was in territory he hadn't climbed that afternoon, forced to make rapid decisions about the route and hoping, rather than knowing, that he was moving in the right direction. He still had his map and his compass but they would be no help until he reached the top.

Soon he heard sounds of others climbing after him. That gave him new purpose and he started to move more quickly, grabbing handfuls of scrub, hauling himself across rocks and patches of mud. And he could tell from the sounds behind him that he was widening the gap between himself and those who were following.

Then he discovered he had chosen the wrong route.

He was beneath an overhang and whether he moved right or left there seemed no way round it. The sensible course would be to back down and try a different path but he wasn't going to yield ground. There was a bush growing out of a crack in the rock above him. He reached up, grabbed a branch with his right hand and swung out with his feet hanging free.

He pushed his left boot in against the rock and manoeuvred its toe into a crack. He pushed down hard on his foot and the toe held firm. He looked around for a hold for his left hand and, as he heaved himself up towards a likely crevice in the rock, two things happened simultaneously: his toe slipped and the branch broke. And then he was falling back, spinning slowly into familiar gloom. But what he couldn't understand was why, once again, he heard that insistent electronic bleep.

At nine-fifteen, the motorcyclist who'd been waiting beside the bridge at Milldale, sitting astride the large old-fashioned Norton, kicked the engine into life. The bike moved slowly up the narrow road by the river, then turned towards the main road to Buxton and the North. Only when it reached the main road did the bike, with its empty pillion seat, accelerate angrily into the rain as if the rider cared little about risk.

Chapter Two

The electronic bleep was getting on his nerves. It wasn't shrill. It wasn't even loud. What got him down was its insistent regularity, as if it were determined to count away every second of his life. It was even beginning to suppress the pleasure of lying between crisp sheets with a well-sprung mattress beneath him, a soft pillow under his head. At first he'd assumed the bleep came from his watch and he'd tried to press the button on his wrist. His left arm was wedged against something on the bed but, when he'd explored the wrist with his other hand, his watch was gone.

Bleep. Bleep. On and on. The time had come for vigorous anti-bleep activity. But what? Not an easy decision. He considered the pros and cons for several minutes before voting in favour of an entrepreneurial initiative. He would open one eye.

He saw a window with grey sky beyond it and a white bar running across it. He refocused on the bar and found it was the rail at the foot of his bed. The cover on his bed, uncreased and neatly laid across him, was also white. The room was full of white. He closed his eye. But the damn bleep still persisted.

He lay still to gather more strength then had a go with both eyes. Yes he was in a hospital room. Couldn't be anything else. He was in bed and was wearing pyjamas of familiar shape and pattern. He didn't need to look at the label. It would read "St Michael".

His left arm wasn't wedged but bandaged to a splint to prevent him from bending his elbow and knocking out the intravenous needle inserted in his vein. The needle was being fed with clear fluid from a half-full plastic pouch suspended from a stand beside his bed. Why hadn't they put the needle into his wrist? It couldn't have been that his watch was in the way. They'd taken that. Why hadn't they used a catheter?

Trying to answer questions was exhausting. And he still didn't know where the bleep was coming from.

Somewhere over his right shoulder. A monitor, he bet. He couldn't turn his head—well, not without giving the pros and cons some careful consideration—but he could squint down his nose and, when he did, he saw wires attached to his chest. That was it. He was being monitored and each bleep signalled a heartbeat. His heart. That made it more reassuring. Operation Bleep Detection successfully completed, he closed both eyes and retreated into sleep.

The next time he woke there was someone in the room. A nurse. As he opened his eyes, she bent over him. Heavily powdered face, a crimson cupid's bow, frizzy overblonde hair under a starched cap, and big blue eyes opened far too widely in a fixed, startled smile.

"Now, now, Dr Marsden," she cooed, "have you decided to join us?" God defend us, she was one of those. He shut his eyes immediately.

"Now, now, now." The cooing had turned to scolding. "We have to wake up some time."

Her voice matched her appearance, which was that of a nurse in a *Carry On* film, though she was just a little too old for the part. Say fifteen years too old.

Bill decided to repay her in her own coin. He slowly opened his eyes, looked up submissively, and spoke.

"Where am I?"

It came out even more throatily than he intended.

"Don't you worry your poor old brain about that," she said. "Doctor says we're on the mend and aren't we lucky we haven't done ourselves any serious damage?"

Oh aren't we lucky indeed. Sorry nurse. I got you wrong. Not so much *Carry On* as 1940s black and white. Didn't I once see you fussing over Franchot Tone?

But Bill was too tired for conversation so he kept his eyes closed and pretended to go back to sleep.

No serious damage, she'd said. Better check on that. He tried each group of muscles and each joint in turn, starting by wiggling his toes, then flexing each ankle, and then each knee. He worked his way through arms and body and finished with the muscles of his face. Realizing the grimaces he was making, he hoped the nurse was watching. But when he opened his eyes she had gone.

Still, nice to know that everything was in working order, apart from his left arm, of course, and the only problem there was that it was tethered to the drip. His head was a bit fuzzy but nothing that some fresh air wouldn't blow away. The muscles of his thighs and calves ached a bit but no more than you'd expect after the walking.

Walking. He'd been walking a lot, and climbing, and Ron was lying on the path, and Bill had fallen. Dovedale. That's where he'd been. What on earth had he been doing there? He'd once gone to Dovedale on a picnic with his parents. Odd place to return to. He'd said goodbye to Tim Craddock and Tim had had tears on his cheeks.

He'd seen police, in cars, on hills with field-glasses, stretched across a valley in a long line, moving slowly forward, stabbing at the undergrowth with sticks as if looking for a dead body, a missing child, a wanted person. But why had he come to Dovedale? Quarrying out memory was too much like hard work. He closed his eyes. The world went black.

He woke suddenly. Frightened. Mouth dry. Electronic bleep accelerating. Fear on its own. Didn't know what he was frightened of. Maybe it was the noise. Low. Threatening. A noise he daren't sleep through.

He turned his head. There were people in the room. Mumbling at the foot of his bed. Was that all? Mumbling?

He turned his head further.

Two people. One was Nurse Sunshine, the other a doctor. Or at least he had a stethoscope hung round his neck. Private practice dress: no white coat but a dark pin-striped suit. Tall, slim, elegant, mid-forties, silvery hair. Central casting again.

The doctor raised his head suddenly and caught his patient peeping at him.

"Glad you decided to join us," he said. Too brisk. Too smooth. Too well fed.

What are you worried about, Marsden? The man's quite civil. Smile at him.

"You're a fortunate fellow," said the pin-striped man. "Tum-

21

bling down rock faces at your time of life. Lucky you didn't land up in the morgue. Must have bounced off some friendly bushes. A few scratches, bruises, mild concussion. We'll have you up tomorrow." The words were all right but there was something odd about the intonation.

You're too suspicious, Marsden. Say something to the gentleman.

"Does that mean I'll be able to go home?"

The doctor threw back his head and snorted a laugh. A hollow laugh. A real laugh?

"Fully recovered, I'd say. Going home's got nothing to do with me. You know more than I do about these people who take so great an interest in your future. Best ask them."

Bill tried to pretend he knew what the doctor was talking about. Some patients, he'd heard, have to do it all the time.

"How long have I been here?"

Did Dr Pin-stripe hesitate before he replied?

"Twenty-four hours of course. Routine observation after concussion. Thursday today. You did your Sherpa Tensing act yesterday. Wednesday. But you know that."

Bill didn't like to admit that he didn't. But given time he could work it out. He tried another probe.

"Bit over the top, isn't it? Saline drip? ECG monitor?"

The doctor laughed.

"Have to look after our own you know. No one else does."

"And how about these important people? When do I see them?"

"I've told them to leave you alone till tomorrow. Meanwhile I think we can unplug you from the mains."

With some help and some hindrance from Nurse Sunshine, he removed the leads from his patient's chest, took down the drip, and put a small plaster over the hole the needle had left in the skin. He then performed a brisk but comprehensive neurological examination: looking at Bill's optic discs, testing for sensory loss, eliciting muscle reflexes.

"Nothing there," he said. "We'll have you up tomorrow. Meanwhile, if I were you, I'd get all the rest I could. If you get any headache, let the nurse know. I'll tell her you can have a couple of soluble aspirins."

22

He picked up reflex hammer, tuning fork, and ophthalmo-scope from the bed and walked to the door. Then he turned.

"Tell me, are you the W. J. Marsden who organized the multicentre trials with recombinant interferon?"

Bill nodded his head in affirmation.

"Thought you might be. Knew Webster and his chums when I was at the Hammersmith."

And before his patient could respond, he was gone.

W. J. Marsden, MD, FRCP, settled back on his pillow and wondered what the hell the man had been talking about. Or maybe he did know and the fall had corrupted the information on a cerebral disc. He needed to sort out what he knew step by step. He turned on his side and slid down under the bedclothes so that if that bloody nurse came back he could look as if he were asleep.

The best place to start was the morning that Craddock greeted him at the Centre. That picture was well-focused. Craddock's enthusiastic smile, the forelock hanging across his forehead, the boyish face.

"Delighted to meet you. Know all about you, of course. Deputed to show you round. Sir Rex said to explain he was sorry he couldn't do it himself but he's had to go up to town to a meeting at the Ministry. Ironic, really, 'cos we've got the new junior minister visiting here. Sir R suggested I show you both round at the same time. Hope you don't mind."

Bill's taxi had been stopped at the main gate and an army sergeant, who appeared to have taken a vow of silence, had transferred his bag to a Land Rover and driven him up the mile-long drive that ran through parkland to the early-Victorian mansion by the lake.

"Bit Edgar Wallace, isn't it?" he said to Craddock. "High-powered research in a country house. All that barbed wire. Armed guard at the gate."

"Wait till you meet the colonel," said Craddock. "If he weren't in charge of security, he'd be locked up in a home for the incurably paranoiac. That's really the only drawback here. We keep tripping over the Official Secrets Act. But the work's good. Unbelievable equipment. No expense spared when you work for the Ministry of Defence. Not like the NHS. And Sir

Rex is a decent old stick. He's delighted to get you because of your experience with clinical trials though what we're up to here is far removed from pharmaceuticals."

The junior minister turned out to be a pleasant young man. No scientific training, of course. It was the first thing he told them, as though boasting of a battle honour. But his advertising agency—"still has my name in the title but of course I've given up any direct financial interest"—had handled scientific accounts.

"You probably remember the corporate campaign we did for General Chemicals, for instance, and I'm sure you remember our television ads for Soothit. Grabbed ten per cent of the indigestion market just like that."

The Soothit commercial had won an award and given him a fascinating insight into the whole world of science.

When Tim Craddock introduced them, the minister shook Bill's hand energetically and nearly withered him with a laser-beam smile.

"Welcome aboard. You're the new chap. Heard all about you. Epidemiologist isn't it? Never quite sure what that means. Always assumed it had to do with influenza, tropical diseases, that sort of thing. Still, I'm sure they'll find you something useful to do here."

New laboratories and mess buildings had been built behind the old house which was now given over largely to administrative offices and the canteen. The basement, however, had been devoted to science and that was where they started their tour. The original cellars had been extended and reinforced with steel pillars and beams.

Their first encounter was with a bank of 100-gallon fermentation vessels, interlinked with so much lagged piping and surrounded by so many valves that they looked like a central heating plant. Indeed that was what the minister thought that they were until Tim explained their true purpose. Elsewhere in the basement they visited a large cold room, part-store and part-laboratory, an analytical electron microscope, a sophisticated radiographic chamber, and a long room containing four twenty-foot-long glass-sided water baths.

Each glass tank was thermostatically controlled and had an

insulating carpet of ping-pong balls floating on its surface. Through the carpet protruded the necks of flasks filled with red nutrient fluid in which human cells, many generations distant from their original progenitor, continued to grow.

From the basement, they went to the new laboratories built in the grounds. These too were equipped to a standard Bill had thought existed only in the catalogues of scientific instrument makers and the fantasies of young scientists. He recognized electronic marvels that could perform sophisticated cytofluorography, measure minute protein concentrations, or monitor each stage of a complex chemical process. And he saw machines which could work more patiently and delicately than any human when drawing out the glass micropipettes which a skilled operator could insert into the nucleus of a cell.

Whenever they paused before one of the marvels, the minister was always more interested in what it cost than what it did, though he was never short of a chirpy phrase for any white-coated workers who raised their eyes from their work to acknowledge the presence of visitors. He was like an army officer who fancied himself at "man management".

The only pieces of technology that really engaged his attention were the computer screens on which chemists using keyboards could create three-dimensional models of new substances and then slowly rotate them to examine their structure.

"Should have brought my young son," he said. "He's a dab hand at computer games."

They met the head of each department, usually in an office which was a mere annexe to a laboratory, and, when Tim Craddock introduced them, Bill tried to guess whom they regarded with the greater suspicion, the minister or himself.

Yet, though the minister showed little interest in the work he actually saw being done, he was eager for information about what he called "background". He started his questioning as they waited for the lift to take them to the basement.

"This DNA stuff, Craddock. Now, tell me all about that."

And as their tour progressed Tim conducted a "listen with Mother" course in biotechnology. Bill was impressed by the way he spelled out the rudiments simply and directly without

25

once sounding condescending. He started by explaining that the molecular chain of DNA was, in truth, the "master plan" of life transmitted from generation to generation. The "plan" consisted of a chain of linked genes, each gene carrying the code for a protein that the organism—human being, plant, single cell—needed in order to live. In humans, for instance, one gene might carry the plan for manufacturing insulin, another the plan for manufacturing a hormone.

"Manufacturing?" asked the minister.

Tim explained that every body cell was a protein factory which could assemble thousands of proteins vital for its survival, and the survival of every other cell in the body. Each cell contained all the components it needed to build each protein and used its own DNA as a template to get the structure right. Now, thanks to the techniques of bioengineering, scientists could programme non-human cells to produce human proteins. And, at the Centre, they'd devised techniques to make bacterial cells, like those the minister had seen growing in the fermentation vessels in the basement, produce complex human proteins which science had no other way of making.

The way the minister egged Tim on suggested he'd decided he might after all get something useful out of this trip round a dreary laboratory. His pumping of Craddock was remorseless and Bill wondered why the man hadn't bothered to read a Janet and John book on biotechnology on the train. But that was probably why Lasersmile was one of Her Majesty's ministers and Bill was doing a job with an enigmatic title. Not that Tim seemed to mind being pumped. Indeed, he appeared to enjoy it.

"Tell me now," said the minister, "what happens when you transfer a human gene into a bacterium?"

The question reminded Bill of the time he was rung up by a researcher on a BBC current affairs programme: "Sorry to bother you, Dr Marsden. We're doing a programme next Friday on 'The Meaning of Life' and we wonder if you have any ideas."

But Tim was away, explaining how a gene from a human cell will act as the code for producing the same protein no matter what cell it happens to be in, human or bacterial, and how the non-human cells used in most of the Centre's experiments were *E coli* bacteria because they'd been studied for so long that we knew more about them than about any other cells. Scientists had already worked out the chemical effects of a third of *E coli*'s two thousand genes, an easier number to cope with than the near hundred thousand found in a human cell.

The vats the minister had seen in the basement contained huge quantities of *E coli* bacteria kept under conditions which encouraged them to grow rapidly. But these were not ordinary *E coli*. Their ancestors had had their nuclei injected with a human gene and now produced the protein the Centre was interested in. The "breakthrough"—the word was the minister's not Tim's—had come when they'd found a way of extracting that protein from the chemical mixture produced by the bacteria. Already they had tried its effects in man and the results were so exciting they wanted to go ahead with a large-scale clinical trial. That was why Dr Marsden was joining them.

And with the entrance of Bill and his strange-sounding speciality, the minister appeared to lose interest. He had to leave at 12.30 to have lunch with local party worthies. Tim and Bill went with him to reception to hand in his visitor's security badge and to see him out through the turnstile gate in the steel grille that ran across the hall just inside the front entrance. The reward for their courtesy was one handpump each and one superlaser beam apiece. As the minister stepped briskly across the outer hall on his way to his official car, they each gave him a dutiful wave through the bars and Bill felt like a long-term prisoner offering a respectful farewell to a tedious prison visitor.

"Let's go and have some lunch in the canteen," said Tim.

The canteen was in a large high room that probably started life as a ballroom. When they'd collected their food from the self-service counter, Tim carried his tray to a table occupied by two contrasting characters. One was a large jovial man, with a plethoric face crowned by an extravagant halo of wavy white hair, who was crammed into an unbuttoned white coat some two sizes too small for him. The other was a sandy-haired man, probably in his mid-thirties, whose forehead and cadaverous cheeks bore a bountiful crop of freckles and who wore no white coat but broad-check lumberjack shirt and jeans.

As Bill approached, the white-haired man stood and extended a pudgy hand.

"You must be Marsden. Shaughnessy. Jim's the name but everybody calls me Paddy. Nice to know you. We missed you on your grand tour because the pair of us took evasive action. This miserable looking sod is Wilkinson who pretends to be a biochemist but is really a professional tennis cheat."

Tim felt compelled to chip in.

"It was Greg Wilkinson's work, of course, that started this whole project and Paddy produced the monoclonal antibodies we use to isolate our mystery protein."

Wilkinson responded with a friendly smile at Bill.

"You a tennis player?" he asked. The accent was unmistakable.

"Queensland?" asked Bill.

Wilkinson nodded. "Brisbane," he said.

"And yes I am a tennis player," said Bill. "I saw the courts when I dumped my bag at the mess. They look good."

"Great courts," said Wilkinson. "No expense spared. It's the motto of this place."

"Whatever you do don't play him for money," said Shaughnessy.

A dark-haired woman wearing a white coat stormed up to their table. Tim tried to introduce her.

"Kate Hutchison. Clinical pharmacologist. In charge of Phase One testing."

Kate gave Bill a quick nod.

"Hi," she said then turned angrily to Wilkinson.

"Who's playing silly buggers with the new batches of IM3? There's a security toad sitting outside the specimen fridge and he won't let me open it without some new sort of pass."

"Give you one guess," drawled Wilkinson. "But there's no point in getting steamed up. They'll give you one at the office if you ask them nicely."

"I wish the pair of you would get steamed up occasionally," said Kate. "This is meant to be a high-powered scientific research unit, but you all seem determined to hand the place over to the security spooks."

She was tall, slim, possibly mid-thirties. Bill was a poor estimator of ages of people younger than himself. Her dark hair was cut short with a fringe over her forehead and one or two spikes stuck out at aberrant angles from the top of her head. Her face was thin, her jaw sharply angled and masculine, and an angry blush suffused the pale skin of her cheeks.

Kate turned to Bill.

"Sorry about that," she said, "but there are times when this place seems to be run for the benefit of everybody except those of us doing the work. Maybe you'll start a new fashion and stand up to the toads. You were at Thomas's, weren't you? William Marsden. Difficult name to forget."

"Don't tell me. I've heard all the jokes, like a schoolboy who's called Winterbottom. No, I didn't found the Royal Free. Nor did I found the cancer hospital."

"But you did marry a friend of mine. Susie and I were in the same year at Cambridge, both at Girton. We tried to keep in touch but she did her clinical in Oxford and I went to George's. We met a few times after we qualified and when she got the job at Tommy's. She told me some things about you that may come in useful if any blackmail is called for."

"That is a class of information no decent woman would keep to herself," said Shaughnessy.

"I was in the States when you married," said Kate, "but we were still writing to one another then so I knew all about it."

Bill tried to interrupt.

"She told me about you too but . . .'

Kate cut in again, a-bubble with enthusiasm.

"Your coming here was the best news I've had in ages. I'm *really* looking forward to seeing her again."

"Susie died five years ago," said Bill.

"Ker-rist!' said Kate. She raised both hands and flattened the palms against her cheeks, fingers splayed and pointing upwards. The narrow strip of face she left visible turned a deepening red and Shaughnessy, good old reliable Shaughnessy, he remembered, told a long story about a surgeon having to tell a patient that he'd amputated the wrong leg.

*

The sky beyond the window had darkened. He had no watch and there was no clock in the room. He rang the push-bell that dangled from the bedside cabinet and, after a minute or two, Nurse Sunshine reappeared, looking even more wide-eyed than he remembered.

"Sorry to bother you," said Bill, "but I haven't a watch and I've no idea of the time."

She looked at the tiny watch pinned to the balcony of white starch constructed over her bosom.

"Golly," she said, "not quite half-four. I guess it looks later because the sky has clouded over."

His brain was clearer now and the nurse was less of a joke. The hardness in the eyes didn't match the fluffiness of the performance. He decided to play along.

"Did my watch survive the fall? It would be nice to have it. It's bad enough not knowing where I am."

She just stared at him. Smiling. But the smile rose no higher than her cheek-bones.

Bill tried again.

"Where on earth is this place anyway?"

She suddenly went into action as if someone had pressed a switch.

"Now, now Doctor Marsden, you should know better than to worry your poor old brain with details like that."

Oversmiling. Overcaring.

"You just give that poor old head of yours time to clear and we'll tell you everything in the morning."

Sally Sunshine, the angel of Ward Three.

She gave an impressive heave to her bosom, and left. It would have been quite in character if she'd blown him a kiss.

Or smashed a fist into his face.

He waited for a minute then slipped his legs over the side of the bed. For a moment he felt light-headed, so he paused. Then he padded across to the door, picking his steps carefully with bare feet across the lino. He turned the handle of the door. It was locked.

He walked to the window. The sky was a seamless grey shroud. A gravel path ran past the window and beyond it lay a scraggy lawn with a circular bed cut at its centre. The bed

30

contained a few rose bushes, which hadn't been pruned this year, and possibly last, set around a sundial which had tilted on its base as though in desperate search of the sun.

Beyond the lawn was an untrimmed hedge, beyond that a field with a fine crop of thistles, and beyond that a distant hill with two bushy trees on the top. The sash-window was screwed immovably into place, and outside it, set in the thick stone walls, were six vertical iron bars covered with a few flakes of yellowing white paint and a lot of brown rust.

He went back to the bed, climbed in, and lay on his side with his back to the window. The question to consider was one he remembered asking himself a lot of times recently. Were the bars on the window there to keep intruders out or to keep the patients in?

Chapter Three

Kate and Bill sat on a sloping bank beside the lake. Behind them the grass had been tamed, rolled, and mown into a smooth striped lawn.

Two huge dragon-flies darted nervously above the water.

"I shudder every time I think of that moment in the canteen," said Kate.

"Maybe I could decondition you by teasing you. Keep harping on about it."

"Do you mind talking about Susie?"

"There aren't many people who want to listen. Except myself."

"I really was very fond of her," said Kate.

"She was of you. Talked a lot about you. Wanted us to meet but she lost track of you."

"I'm lousy at keeping in touch with people I like. And Susie was one of those friends you didn't have to keep on meeting. No matter how long since we met, we could always pick up just where we left off. What happened?"

"CA of the ovary. Whoops. Sounds as though I'm trotting out the diagnosis to a medical audience. But that's what it was. She spent the last two months in a hospice. No pain. It was the happiest time we had together. The night before she died, we went out to a concert and had dinner afterwards. During dinner, she said: 'How awful it would have been if I'd fallen under a bus. I'd never have had this time to find out about myself, about what really counts in life, and about you."

Kate placed her right hand flat against her neck then let it slide slowly down her skin till it lay in the gap between her breasts. The air was still. A distant shout of joy came from the tennis courts at the far side of the house.

"I reckon you're a lucky lad," she said.

Then she shook her head as if to reshuffle its contents.

"What the hell brings you here?" she asked. "Not at all your sort of place I'd have thought."

"It seemed an interesting job. Something different. When Sir Rex approached me he made it sound exciting."

"Come off it. This isn't an interview. You've already got the job. Sexy Rexy's personal choice. I find the whole place spooky."

"I wish my head wasn't so fuzzy," he said. "Maybe I should ring for Sally Sunshine and ask for those soluble aspirin."

"For who?" asked Kate.

"No one you know."

Kate lay back against the bank and gazed at the sky. She wore a yellow-linen jump suit, with the upper buttons undone, and the masculinity of the urchin head was at odds with the ultramarine fingernails and the soft skin shadowed by the gaping collar.

"I really do feel very sad about Susie," she said. "Isn't it awful the way you can lose whole chunks of the life you intended to lead. Susie was always going to be there when I got round to looking her up. Yet, while I was busy staring in another direction, someone sneaked in behind my back and buggered up your world."

Another moment of stillness. Another echo from the tennis court.

"In two years' time," said Kate, "I'm going to be forty, and I still haven't got used to the idea of being thirty."

"Two years ago I was fifty," said Bill. "I found it relatively painless. I even gave a party."

Her gaze was still fixed on the sky and she spoke without looking at him.

"Susie was lucky. Luckier than I'll ever be. I reckon the pair of you were right lucky sods."

Then she rolled on to her side to face him and produced an impetuous grin.

"Take me out to dinner tonight," she said. "I fancy an evening with a dirty old man."

One of the dragon-flies darted over Bill's head. As he turned to watch it, a sound came from the centre of the lake. An insistent worrying sound. Dry bones rattling. Louder and more agitated. Then the dragon-fly darted again and the world turned black.

Bill looked back. Too late. He knew that Kate was gone, that he was alone, and now the darkness was impenetrable. Rattling noise. Key in lock. Rattling key.

The light came on so blindingly that he couldn't stop blinking. Sally Sunshine stood in the doorway.

"Wakey, wakey," she half sang. "We've got a visitor. A very special visitor, indeed."

And there stood Sir Rex Copeland. But was it Rex or an inflated doll? The right shape: short, broad shouldered, and incipiently corpulent. The right glued-on extras: short grey hair as neatly parted and as smoothly brushed as the thin grey moustache. And dressed like Rex. Dark suit and an old something-or-others tie. The doll came to life and crossed the room with hand extended.

"My dear Marsden. Falling down cliffs at your time of life. I thought you'd passed the age of indiscretion. Good to find you in such reasonable fettle."

The vowels were a mite flattened and the manner a mite too affected. How could Kate have ever thought of him as Sexy Rexy? Bill found it odd shaking hands while sitting up in bed.

Rex placed the hat he'd been carrying, broad-brimmed black felt, carefully upon a stool. He was the most dedicated social signaller Bill had ever known. The hat had been chosen, Bill was sure, to proclaim that its owner wasn't a run-of-the-mill stuffed shirt but something of an intellectual; just as, in different company, the tie and suit would proclaim he wasn't one of these sloppy intellectuals but a brisk man of affairs.

Having placed his symbol in a safe place, Sir Rex drew up the room's only chair, an old leather armchair, oversprung and understuffed.

"Thank you, sister," he said, and Sally Sunshine left them, closing the door behind her.

"They looking after you all right?"

"Not much looking after to be done. A nice enough doctor came and saw me and that nurse seems happy to answer the bell, though I doubt she is capable of much else. One thing I'd like to know is where I am."

"This place is run by the department. Comes in useful on occasions. First-class facilities. First-class people. I'll have the nurse changed if you want."

"What I really wondered was what part of the country I was in. Nobody seems prepared to tell me."

"Derbyshire of course. Where you fell. No mystery about that."

Those small eyes, which looked so innocuous from afar, could sometimes, just momentarily, reveal something of the complex organism within the well-trimmed shell. Now they rested unblinking on Bill. Bill shrugged.

"Lucky you had a bed so close by," he said. "Now all I need to know is what I was doing in Derbyshire."

"We just want you to get fit again. No need to come rushing back to work. We can just about manage without you."

A thin smile creased Rex's face and vanished as swiftly as it had appeared.

"Kate Hutchison is preparing the data for a presentation to our lords and masters. No problem there. We've all played devil's advocate and tried to find a flaw in your figures but we can't. It looks as though we have a spectacular success on our hands."

Bill wondered what the hell he was talking about.

"Still. Mustn't start you working again. Not till you get the all-clear from them here. Just thought you'd like to know everything was under control. Real object of the visit is to make sure they are looking after you properly. See if there's anything I can do. Would you really like me to get them to change the nurse?"

"Don't bother. She's quite entertaining. When can I get out of here?"

"Better ask them dear boy. I've no clinical responsibility here. Just as well. Can't have clinical decisions taken by your boss. The great thing is not to come rushing back too soon."

Another quick thin smile.

"We really can manage for the time being. Though all of us are, of course, looking forward to having you back."

He stood and Bill once again found himself awkwardly shaking hands.

Sir Rex carefully retrieved his hat, walked to the door and tapped it gently with his knuckles. It opened immediately as if someone had been standing there waiting for the knock. Sir Rex turned to face Bill.

"Good to see you, dear boy. I'll tell them all you look a picture of health."

Sally Sunshine, who stood behind him, moved to one side and he was gone. She crossed the room and switched on the lamp on the bedside table.

"Now, don't you fall asleep," she said. "I'll be back soon with your supper."

"Your name isn't Sally, is it?"

Her eyes, he felt sure, would have opened even wider if they weren't already fully extended.

"Whatever gave you that idea?"

She gave another heave to the starched balcony and, as she left, turned off the main light. After she'd closed the door, Bill heard the key turn in the lock.

He couldn't make head nor tail of Rex's visit. Maybe he'd dreamed it. Then he saw the leather chair beside his bed. Dreams don't move the furniture around. He slid down under the bedclothes.

A fox walked across his line of sight. A thin, mangey-looking animal. But indubitably a fox. Suddenly it saw Bill and froze, standing quite still and staring at him. Its eyes were dark and moist and the stare unwavering. Then it slowly turned its head and walked towards the steel gate. There was someone at the gate, opening it. Bill stretched his head round trying to see who was there but they stayed just beyond his range of vision, turning the key noisily in the lock.

For the second time, the rattling of the key awakened him. The door reopened, and Sally Sunshine entered with his supper on a tray. He was already watching her and caught the hard eyes before she could embed them in a smile.

"Let's see you sit up straight in bed," she said.

She placed the tray on a bedtable and rolled it forward from the foot of the bed till it was under his chin.

"Now doesn't that look nice and tasty?"

He silently pleaded the fifth amendment.

36

"If there's anything more you want, just ring."

And she was gone.

It was like a school meal. A few slices of tinned grapefruit in a glass bowl, soaked with syrup and topped with a dry-looking cherry that had once been *glacé*; a large white plate bearing a small slice of cold ham, an overbaked potato, and some glutinous coleslaw. The only refreshing aspects of the view were a teapot under a woollen cosy, a strainer, and slices of lemon in a saucer. He poured himself a cup of tea, rolled up the slice of ham and dispatched it in one swallow, picked with his fork at the potato, and wondered how they knew he didn't take sugar and preferred not to take milk.

While he sipped, he re-examined the available pieces of the jigsaw that was once his memory. He remembered the fall, and the eighteenth-century dean, and a man he'd knocked over on a path. Beyond that there was a gap, though he knew the fall came when he was walking through Dovedale where he'd once been on a picnic with his parents. But trying to recall facts before the eighteenth-century dean made him feel panicky. He generated less anxiety when he approached the gap from the other side. The Centre, for instance. His memory of that was clear and he'd been doing quite well trying to bridge forward from there. That was the way to go, but he had to move slowly.

He dug out another forkful of potato. It was dry and tasteless. He tried the coleslaw. It tasted of the plastic tub from which it had been tipped. He threw down his fork in disgust. The key rattled in the door and in came Sally busily assembling another wide-eyed smile.

"Enjoyed our supper, did we?"

She looked at the plate.

"Not interested in our food, are we. We won't get better quickly, now, if we don't take nourishment."

"We'll try to do better in the morning," he said, as solemnly as he could. He doubted she'd detect an innuendo if he hit her over the head with it.

"Time to settle down for bye-byes," said Sally.

She moved the bedtable back to the foot of the bed, pulled a blue blind down over the window, and plumped up his pillows.

"Sleep tight," she said. "And let's hope we feel better in the morning. We can always ring the bell if we have problems."

Then she gathered up the tray, carried it across the room, and balanced it precariously on one hand while she opened the door and squeezed through. Before she closed the door behind her, she paused and sent the day's last flash of eyes and teeth over her shoulder. Bill waited for the crash outside but it didn't come. Damn. He meant to ask her if there were any books in the place. He didn't feel sleepy and he didn't want to lie staring at the ceiling and brooding. He'd had enough digging at memory for today.

He decided to wait for a bit, then try the bell and see if the night nurse was any improvement on the day one. Watch carefully when she came in and see if he could catch her before she switched on. Easier to catch them switching on than switching off. Never caught Sunshine switching off. Her exits were very deliberate, a set routine. But there'd been something different about her last one. She'd been carrying the tray . . .

He slipped his legs out of bed and padded to the door. He turned the handle slowly and pulled it towards him. The door moved, unlocked. That was what had been different. She'd got in such a muddle carrying the tray she'd forgotten to lock the door.

Back in bed, he leaned against his pillows. He'd best wait for a bit. How long? An hour. How would he know when an hour was up? They still hadn't returned his watch and he had no idea what time it was, save that now it was dark outside. The night nurse would probably check the lock when she came on. So he couldn't leave it too long.

He decided to allow Sunshine time to settle elsewhere, bringing a little light into other patients' lives—and to forget she hadn't locked the door. He'd count to a hundred slowly. One . . . two . . . three . . . The counting stirred a memory. Counting raindrops under a bush. Surely not. Yet the memory came through clearly. He dismissed it brusquely. No time now for distraction. He'd been handed a chance that he doubted would be repeated. Seventeen . . . eighteen . . .

Ninety-eight . . . ninety-nine . . . She hadn't returned. No rattle of key in lock. He got out of bed again and looked

38

around the room hoping he might see a pair of slippers. He opened the door of the bedside locker. No slippers but there was his watch, and his wallet, and his loose change. A neatly folded towel, soap, toothbrush, toothpaste, and disposable razor. What a fool not to have thought of looking there before.

He looked at the watch—it was five to ten—and strapped it to his wrist. Then he padded once more across the room, turned the door handle, and pulled it towards him as gently as he could. It opened without a squeak. As he stepped through the door, the texture beneath his feet changed from linoleum to polished wood block. He was in a large dark space. The only light came from his bedside lamp spilling through the door behind him.

He pulled the door to and, as his eyes accommodated, found it easier to see. Light from outside, too bright for moonlight, came through a tall window to his right. He was in a large high-ceilinged hall, panelled in dark wood, and a staircase with an elaborately carved balustrade ascended past the window on his right. He felt he'd strayed on to the set of a Ben Travers farce. It would surprise him not at all to find a suit of armour standing in the corner.

To his left was a heavy door, similar to the one through which he'd come, and beyond that a large fireplace with, Lord love us, an ostentatious coat of arms carved above the mantel. Beyond the fireplace was another door, and two more in the wall facing him. He wondered through which Ralph Lynn and Robertson Hare would make their entrance. Now he understood where Sunshine came from. She would lose her uniform in reel three and run up the staircase in her slip. He was in one of those 1930s British movies shown on Channel 4 on a Saturday afternoon.

He tried the door on his left. It opened easily and he looked inside. Again golden light from outside came through the window. The room was a narrow office: a desk, filing cabinet, wire trays piled higgledy-piggledy on a stack of cardboard cartons. Not very medical. He closed the door and took another look around the hall. This time he could see light under the door directly opposite. Probably sister's office. He'd leave that till last.

The next door on the left beyond the fireplace would be a ward or perhaps another private room. He listened outside it. Silence. He tried the handle. It turned noiselessly and the door yielded to his pressure. Beyond was a familiar pattern of golden light and dark shadow. No ward this. A large drawing-room with furniture covered with dust sheets. The far corner of the room was the far corner of the house and the golden light came through uncurtained windows in both walls. The penny dropped. The house was floodlit.

He closed the door and stood for a moment in the hall. Then, circling wide around the door that showed bright, ungolden, light beneath it, he tried each of the other doors in turn. Only one was locked and behind the others he found one dust-sheeted dining-room, one dust-sheeted billiards-room, one dust-sheeted room of indeterminate purpose—possibly a morning-room but difficult to see because it was the only one not bathed in golden light. A cupboard under the stairs yielded a clutter of raincoats, hats, wellies, umbrellas, walking-sticks, and a bag of rusty-looking golf clubs.

He had found no bathroom, no lavatory, no sluice, no dispensary, no sign of any other patient, no sign indeed that this was any sort of medical establishment.

Of the room he'd seen, only one seemed worthy of further investigation. He walked softly back across the hall and re-entered the office, closing the door behind him. He ferreted first through the cartons on the floor and found them filled with batches of dusty stationery that had been tipped into them.

Next he tried the filing cabinet. The top drawer squeaked as he pulled it out and, as it squeaked, he heard a noise in the hall. He left the cabinet and stood by the door listening. Someone was crossing the hall, thin heels tapping on the wooden blocks. For a moment he couldn't remember whether he'd closed the door of his room. If he hadn't, it was too late now. The footsteps halted and then he heard the front door being opened. There was a sound of voices and then the door slammed shut. Silence. He waited for a minute then opened the office door just a crack. The hall was empty and his door *was* closed. He reclosed the office door and returned to the filing cabinet.

The cabinet was as unhelpful as the cartons. The top three drawers were empty and the bottom one was stacked with copies of *Country Life* and *Vogue*. When he held a random sample up to the golden light, he discovered they were all dated 1973.

He next tried the desk. One end was supported on steel legs, the other on a steel pedestal that had three drawers built into it. The top one, shallow, contained pencils various, a pair of scissors, an old brown envelope and a fine collection of rubber bands. The middle drawer, less shallow, contained a Royal Mail guide to postal rates in 1974, more rubber bands, and even more paper-clips. The third drawer, deep, was packed with typed documents. He dug them out and found they were stapled and rubber-banded into four bundles. The top page of each had been stamped with a single word spelled out in large capital letters: "SECRET".

He held the first bundle up to the light and, as he screwed up his eyes to decipher the closely typed lines, he discovered he was reading Operational Instructions issued to the Red Army for a territorial exercise on Salisbury Plain in 1956. The second bundle was Instructions to Umpires, the third was the briefing for the Blue Army, the fourth was the Umpires' Report. He turned to the back page and read the last paragraph. The Blues it seemed had put up a good show.

He packed the bundles of paper back into the drawer and closed it. Before leaving the desk, he reopened the top drawer and took out the brown envelope. It was unsealed and, when he opened it, the golden light fell on its contents, a small wad of bank notes, five-pounds and ten-pounds. He turned the envelope over and saw that someone had pencilled "£235" on the front of it.

He gazed thoughtfully at his treasure trove for a moment, then tucked back the flap of the envelope and returned it to the drawer.

He crossed to the door and, hearing nothing outside, went into the hall. There was only one room he hadn't investigated, the one on the far side with the bright light shining under the door. He crept across the hall and listened outside it.

He thought he heard two voices. He diagnosed one as Sally

Sunshine though he couldn't hear a word she was saying. She was probably telling a story because her voice went on and on and when she finished on a rising cadence she broke into a cawing laugh. Then came the other voice speaking slow, monotonous, drawn-out sentences. The words were inaudible but their sound provoked a bizarre physical response from the listener in the hall. His skin suddenly turned cold and moist, his heart pounded, and he started to overbreathe. He was seized with a feeling of impending dissolution. The voice terrified him. Fighting to keep a grip on consciousness, he dragged himself back across the hall and into his room. He was now shivering violently but he managed to close the door behind him and crawl into bed.

The shivering seemed uncontrollable. He tried to take deep regular breaths. At first he found it impossible, then he managed one, then two, and then, as his breathing came under control, the shivering slowed and disappeared. He lay back on his pillows, wiped the moisture from his forehead with his hand, closed his eyes, and tried to relax. Slowly the panic eased out of him and he worked hard at assembling some rational thoughts.

Only one thing was certain. It wasn't words that had terrified him but the sound of a voice.

Yet he had no idea to whom the voice belonged.

Chapter Four

He switched off the bedside light. If they saw no light under his door, they'd think he was asleep. He didn't want a visitation and light would attract Madame Sunshine like a moth. Not that he thought of her as Sally Sunshine any more. His picture of her now was of a blowzy blonde sprawled in a leather armchair in the room across the hall, legs dangling over the arm, starched cap askew, lipstick smeared, a cigarette in one hand, glass of gin in the other. No nurse she. Or was he just unleashing a prejudice? The doctor had seemed real enough. And there was no denying the actuality of Sir Rex.

Now that the room was dark, he could see there was no golden light beyond the window blind; just as there had been none in the room he'd decided was the morning-room. This side of the house was not floodlit. Probably for his benefit. They wanted to keep up the illusion of a hospital or nursing home.

Odd that so many people were frightened of the dark. He was reassured by it. Sitting there, undistracted by the detail of the theatrical set in which he seemed to be living, he found it easier to think calmly about what he had discovered in the past half-hour.

First the good news. That panic attack had given a good shake to the databank that held his memory and had cleared some of the confusion. He now could remember what had happened before the fall: the walk along the Manifold River, Ilam Hall, the police, the scramble up the slope.

The not so good news was that he didn't know why Ron had turned on him, or what he had done to be hunted by police. And where were the police now? Maybe he'd lost his marbles and they'd locked him up in a clinic for his own good, entrusting him to the care of his old boss. Yet whatever this place might be, it certainly wasn't a clinic.

As he tried to unravel the possibilities, he felt the panic start to stir within him. Best leave reasons for the time being. The search for them seemed to block his memory. There'd be time for reasons later. First he had to cope with the worst news of all. The voice. He didn't recognize it. He didn't understand it. But its presence meant he had to get away from this place. And quickly. The voice was why he had slept under hedges, hidden from police, knocked over Ron, tried to climb rocks. And the voice was why he had fallen.

The way to keep panic at bay was to forget about the voice and convene a meeting of the escape committee. And as he assembled the committee members—each of them a fact that might be turned to useful purpose—he experienced a surge of confidence. He was doing something that had been a familiar routine in the recent past. It was a declaration of optimism. Don't dig at the memories, now. Call the committee to order. Stick to the agenda. It took but five minutes of dedicated committee work to create a workable plan. He then spent another five minutes trying to destroy it with critical scrutiny. The plan survived. It was time to cross the starting line.

First, he felt around inside the bedside locker till he found his wallet. He took it out and sorted through its contents with his fingers. He removed the three banknotes that he found but left the credit cards and driving licence. He put the banknotes in the breast pocket of his pyjamas and put the wallet back in the locker. As he did so, he gathered the loose change from the floor of the locker and put it in his breast pocket with the banknotes. Then he slipped his legs over the side of the bed and padded to the door. He opened it a crack and took a look at the hall. It was unchanged. Light still showed under the door opposite but, at this distance, he could hear no voices.

He walked softly across the hall to destination number one: the cupboard under the stairs. There, he started with the wellies, and the first pair he tried proved a reasonable fit. He kept them on, tucking his pyjama trousers down inside them. He hoped the wellies were green. Couldn't be sure in this golden light. Green would add a touch of class.

As would the tweed cap he found. Captain Mark Phillips at your service, ma'am.

From the coats he chose a well-worn riding mac and was about to close the cupboard door when he had an afterthought. He took another look inside and selected himself a walking-stick. It was a cheap, unvarnished stick but its handle fitted comfortably into his palm and gave him the sort of reassurance a man can draw from the clasp of a friend.

He feared that the wellies might squeak on the wooden floor but, when he crossed the hall, they made no more noise than had his bare feet. He entered the narrow office, closing the door behind him. There he had light from the window to help him and he went straight to the top drawer of the desk. First he took out the scissors and put them in a pocket of his raincoat. Then he took out the brown envelope, removed the banknotes, and stuffed them in another pocket. He returned the empty envelope to the drawer, and, after he'd closed it, went back to the door and listened. No sound outside. He opened the door and recrossed the hall, picking each step carefully and shoul-dering arms with his walking-stick. He was struck by the incongruity of the sight that would confront anyone who flung open the door of the lighted room. No time now to dwell on frivolity because he faced the only gamble that the plan involved. He went into the "morning-room", closing the door behind him. He had to wait for a moment for his eyes to accommodate to the darkness, then he picked his way carefully past the dust-sheeted furniture towards the faint outline of the window in the far wall. It was a sash-window. He undid the catch and tried to raise the lower half. It slid up easily. He wouldn't need the scissors after all.

He swung himself over the sill and again was struck by the incongruity. Captain Mark Phillips making an unorthodox exit. He stood on grass. If the window was rigged with an alarm, it would be sounding somewhere now. But not here. The house remained silent behind him. He took a few tentative paces forward. He was still walking on grass and there was enough light for him to pick his steps. He glanced back and saw that his previous surmise had been correct. The house was floodlit on three sides but not on this. The lights on the far side gave a golden halo to the silhouette—a silhouette oddly in accord with his memory of the house on the hill in Hitchcock's *Psycho*. He turned his back on memory and walked as swiftly as he could, moving at a right angle from the house, reckoning that was where he would find the deepest shadow.

He was walking on what had once been a lawn but was now well on the way to being a rough field. The wellies were looser than they'd felt when he first put them on, and they rubbed against his heels at every step. If he tried to run they would surely trip him. So he stepped out briskly, swinging his stick as if on an invigorating country walk.

Twenty yards and still no sound behind him. Thirty. Forty. And then he heard them. He stood still and there was silence. He moved forward again and, as he slowly picked each step, he heard soft footsteps on the grass behind him. He turned, raising his stick. Again the steps stopped. Bill felt no panic. This was real and he was prepared to fight. He stood quite still and soon the footsteps restarted. He heard them clearly now, maybe twenty yards away. Then suddenly they accelerated and out of the dark loomed a large Old English sheep-dog. It trotted up to him, licked his hand, and growled contentedly as it rubbed against his legs.

Bill turned and continued his walk. The dog followed. At least it didn't bark. It just seemed happy to have found a chum to share the loneliness of the night. Or maybe the mac or the wellies carried a familiar scent. The dog was large and hairy and bore a more than passing resemblance to one which advertised paint in television commercials. Bill decided to call him Busby.

The lawn-cum-field stretched on and on. Bill suspected he was walking across parkland. He grew better at controlling the wayward boots and a jauntiness entered his step. One man and his dog out for a stroll around the estate. He doffed his cap at a passer-by. Good afternoon, vicar, what a lot of weather we've been having. And then suddenly he was flying through the air. He hovered, twisted, and then crashed into muddy ground. He lay winded on the mud for a minute or two and Busby came and licked his face.

He hauled himself stiffly to his feet and waggled his arms and legs. No grievous damage. He looked back and saw that his invigorating step had carried him straight over the edge of a ha-ha.

He moved on with greater circumspection and with Busby still trotting cheerfully behind. They came to a wood. His inclination was to skirt round it but it seemed familiar territory to Busby who trotted straight up to a patch of scrub, plunged through it, and then stood, tail wagging, on a narrow path beyond. Bill followed. He couldn't think of anything better to do. Once he reached the path, Busby padded off along it. It was dark under the trees but Busby wasn't difficult to follow and, whenever he wandered too far ahead, he stood and waited for Bill to catch up. Occasionally he paused when the path divided, as if deciding which route to take. After ten minutes, Bill realized what a fool he'd been. They were probably going round in circles and this damned dog might well lead him back to the house. Yet he had little choice now but to follow it. He didn't fancy his chances of finding his own way out of the wood while it was dark. And once it was light, it would be too late.

Busby paused at the centre of a clearing. The moon emerged from behind a bank of cloud and Bill saw he was in mixed forest. Silver birches glistened like stage props around the edge of the clearing and beyond them he could see oak and yew and beech. The clearing looked as unreal and theatrical as the backdrop for a romantic ballet. He looked up at the sky and saw that it had cleared save for a few bundles of cloud that an unseen wind was whisking rapidly away. It was going to be a clear night. The air was still chill but maybe the dawn would bring a warm and sunny day. In which case his costume was going to look a touch bizarre. He looked at his watch. One-thirty. Dawn last week came around 5 a.m. He would like to get many more miles between him and his vacated bed before daylight.

Busby was on his way again and Bill followed. He caught an occasional glimpse of the moon through the tops of the trees and was able to reassure himself they were not moving in a circle. They were moving as near as dammit in a straight line, though it could, of course, be a straight line back to the house. Yet even as he happened upon that depressing thought, Busby stopped in front of a large bush. When Bill caught up with him, he turned and licked Bill's hand.

"Good boy," said Bill. "On you go."

Busby stood still and gave Bill's hand another lick. Bill took a closer look at the bush and saw that beyond it was a wooden fence. He pushed his way up to the fence and found he was alongside a road which ran through the wood. Busby stayed behind him on the path.

"Aren't you coming any further?" asked Bill.

He would have liked to think that Busby shook his head. He didn't but his intention was clear; he stood there wagging his tail but not moving forward.

"Well, thanks anyway for bringing me this far. Maybe we should get you a brandy barrel."

Busby wagged his tail more vigorously.

Then he gave a quiet yelp, turned round, and disappeared back into the wood.

Bill climbed the fence on to the road. Left or right? Maybe he should spin a coin but the instinct which his mother used to call his "bump of direction" suggested that turning left would lead him away from the house. So that was the way he went, flopping along in his wellies.

It was hard work. He seemed low on energy and his feet were getting sore. He wouldn't be able to manage many more miles in these boots, even if he had the benefit of socks. Then he heard a car engine, distant at first but growing closer, and quite definitely approaching along the road behind him.

His immediate reaction was to jump into the ditch. They would have found his empty bed by now and would surely start searching local roads. Then he had second thoughts. If they were looking for him, he wouldn't be able to hide for long. He could get in the ditch now but they'd be back in daylight and by then he would be as good as crippled. But if this *wasn't* them, he might be able to hitch a lift. It was his only real hope.

He decided to take the gamble. The loom of lights came over the trees behind him and, seconds later, he saw the lights themselves picking out the road. He turned to face them and started thumbing a lift. The lights came up to him, then passed, and he saw that they belonged to a heavy lorry. It started to

48

slow and pulled up about twenty yards ahead of him. He trotted up to it, flop, flop, flop in his boots.

The driver stuck his head out the window.

"Which way are you heading, squire?"

Bill heard himself answer, "North."

"Doncaster any good to you?"

"Perfect."

"Hop in then."

Bill walked round the front of the lorry and got in through the passenger door.

The driver established noisy engagement between engine and gear-box and the lorry moved off.

Light spilled into the hall as the blonde nurse opened the door. She crossed to her patient's door, opened it slightly and listened. After a pause, she opened it a little wider and listened again. Then she switched on the main light and saw the empty bed. She left the bedroom, opened the door of the office, and turned on the light. She went straight to the desk, opened the top drawer, and picked out the envelope. She checked that it was empty and threw it on the desk. Then she went back across the hall and, as she re-entered the room from which she had emerged, she spoke to someone who was waiting there.

"He's on his way," she said.

Chapter Five

The air in the cab was warm and heavy and reeked of tobacco smoke. The driver's window was fully open; the window alongside Bill was closed.

"Do you mind if I wind this down?" asked Bill.

"Be my guest," said the driver.

They emerged from the wood and passed a row of cottages with a solitary street lamp on the pavement in front of them. The lamp was a useful marker and Bill found that, if he leaned slightly to his right, the large mirror outside the driver's window gave him a good view of the road behind. For the moment, the only light in the mirror was the receding street lamp.

The driver was in his early thirties. He wore a grubby pair of jeans and a black running vest which allowed a flamboyant display of chest hair and bulging shoulder muscle. Yet his thin face and his long dark hair brushed artlessly back from his forehead suggested more a university don than a lorry driver. His accent revealed no more than that at some time he had lived in England's south-eastern enclave.

He cast an amused glanced at Bill.

"You're an odd cove to find walking around in the middle of the night. Let me take a guess; you needn't tell me if I'm right. You look like a man who's come unstuck in a leg-over situation."

Bill smiled a confabulatory smile. The driver's explanation was better than any of those he'd been urgently concocting.

"Did she kick you out of bed or did her husband come home and find you in the wardrobe?"

"I found him in the wardrobe."

The driver laughed.

"A gentleman's offence," he said. "No indecency attached to that. Not like mine. Have a guess what's in the back of this truck?"

Bill sought hard for an outrageous answer.

"Drugs?"

The driver laughed again.

"In a manner of speaking. Opium for the people. In tabloid form. Plenty of bum and tit, false news, and simulated outrage. All hurried through the night by cowboys like me. Now that *is* an indecent offence."

"Then why commit it?"

"I can give you three million good reasons. Or are there four or five million out of work now? We don't really know since she let those creative accountants loose on the books."

He manoeuvred the gear-lever and they slowed. He manoeuvred it again and they started to lumber up a steep hill.

"I've been on the dole," he said, "and even this is better than sitting at home sniffing your armpits."

He took a cigarette from a packet on the ledge in front of him and lit it with the electric lighter from the dashboard. Bill's eyes were still on the mirror. A pair of headlights had taken up constant station three hundred yards behind them on the hill.

"What line are you in?" asked the driver.

"A scientist." A less likely source of supplementaries than "a doctor".

The driver took a deep drag at his cigarette.

"Wouldn't mind being a scientist. Cuts the opportunities for self-deception."

"I wouldn't be so sure," said Bill. "We just deceive ourselves in more sophisticated ways. Rationalization it's called. I work with people who are masters of it."

"Don't we all?"

They'd reached the top of the hill. The driver switched his lights to full beam and lit up a long straight stretch of road ahead. The headlights in the mirror moved closer. Then suddenly they accelerated, and swung out to overtake. Bill found himself shrinking into his seat as if he could hide in one of the cracks in the upholstery. There was a roar of engine beyond the driver's window and Bill couldn't restrain his head from turning to look. Alongside them was a battered old quarter-tonner piled high with cardboard boxes that bounced and swayed as the truck rattled along at its maximum speed. In the cab was one dark figure who gave a wave as he went by.

"Bloody cowboy," said Bill's driver. "He'll be lucky if he doesn't lose that load."

Then he leaned forward, switched on the radio, and twiddled the tuning knob until he found some music. Traditional jazz. The Firehouse Five plus One. Ahead, only one of the quarter-tonner's rear-lights was working and it now receded winking into the distance. In the mirror, the road behind was clear.

The cigarette smoke began to make Bill feel sick. He moved his head closer to the open window, rested his cheek against the door-frame and let the wind blow across his face. He closed his eyes and pretended to sleep.

Rationalization it's called. I work with people who are masters of it.

When he'd first heard about the change in the protocol he'd gone to see Sir Rex.

"My dear Bill, of course you should have been consulted. Can't think how it could have happened. But this business of patients giving informed consent to experimental treatment is not as simple as it looks. I mean, how do we define informed? Is every patient going to have to take an Open University degree in biotechnology? If not, how else can you get them to understand?"

Rex's fingers were entwined across his belly. He looked like an alderman having his portrait painted.

"What we're doing," he said, "is a bit more complicated than a flu jab. And if they only partly understood, we could be subjecting them to a lot of unnecessary anxiety."

"Not to mention making it even more difficult for ourselves to find recruits."

If Rex noticed Bill's acerbity, he wasn't letting on.

"That too. Though, of course, it's not a consideration we would let play any part in our decision. I'm sure you've noticed there's been a lot about informed consent in the journals recently. Indeed, there's a file in the office. I'll get Ann to send you some photocopies. It's one of those professional matters that always look so easy to outsiders. But, of course, it's not. Indeed I'm not convinced that anybody can be *truly* informed.

In my own view we are better off relying on the good sense of the clinicians. There are, after all, lots of people who just don't want to be informed."

Those calculating eyes had been monitoring Bill's reactions.

"But it really is outrageous that the protocol was altered without you being consulted. Security had no right to intervene. Quite, quite outrageous. I'll take it up at the next meeting of the executive committee and you can be assured I shall put your point most vigorously."

Rex was highly intelligent and had a neat and methodical mind. Yet his most valuable gift was an ability to produce an unselfconscious stream of this sort of verbiage. Indeed Bill had decided some time ago that the secret of his success was that he literally "made the right noises". He always *sounded* as though what he was saying was fair and carefully considered, even wise, and in committees he would often keep on spouting till his audience ceased to catch the meaning of the words and just absorbed the flavour of the sound.

The trial had gone ahead, of course, using the protocol rewritten by Security and without patients being told they were part of an experiment. Bill didn't realize it then but the harbinger had ridden into town and the army of ill-fortune was riding close behind.

But, at least, the anger generated by his memory of the interview with Rex had cleared his nausea.

The lorry was slowing. Bill took a quick look in the mirror. The road was clear, but there was a lot of light ahead.

The driver noticed him stir.

"Just coming up to the M1," he said.

Two cars flashed across their bows as they entered the motorway. Bill kept his eyes on the mirror. One car came up behind them in the fast lane and overtook. Then nothing.

The driver snatched a look at him.

"Trying to get some kip? Have an eyes-down now. I'll give you a nudge when we get to Woodall. I'm stopping off there for a quick tea and a bun."

Bill closed his eyes again. When he'd climbed into the cab he'd taken off the Mark Phillips; now he replaced it over the top part of his face to act as an eye-shield. He gained nothing by watching the mirror. If he was followed, he was followed and he couldn't do much about it on the motorway. He really was weary and the cab no longer swayed as they vibrated their way through the night, holding a steady course along the inside lane.

He tried to empty his mind but Sir Rex wasn't going to let him sleep.

They'd all received an urgent summons and sat round the rosewood table in the boardroom, intruders on territory far from their natural habitat. Except for Rex, of course. He sat at the head with a worried-looking Craddock on his right. Next to Craddock sat Kate, then Shaughnessy. Greg Wilkinson sat on Rex's left with Bill alongside him.

Rex opened the copy of the *Lancet* that lay on the table in front of him.

"Let me stress that this is a purely informal meeting. No record will be taken; no minute will result. I think it useful, though, for us to get together. Here at the Centre, we work as part of a team with members of other disciplines and, of course, all of us are very happy to do so. But each of us here this evening is also a member of a profession which lays particular responsibilities upon its members."

"Nice of you to count me in," said Greg. "Never seen a patient since I qualified. I doubt I could deal competently with a verruca."

Rex was impatient with the interruption. He looked at Greg with eyebrows raised in theatrical surprise. Only when he had stared the colonial into submission did he lower his gaze. Then he tapped the open *Lancet* with the backs of two fingers.

"This, of course, is a flagrant breach of the Official Secrets Act which, I would remind you, every one of you signed when you first came here. That aspect will be dealt with appropriately by the authorities and I will dwell on it no further. What concerns me is the way this matter may reflect upon our profession. Up to now we have been accepted as valuable, indeed privileged, members of the team. Let me remind you there was no need for the director of the project to be a physician, and I am aware of the honour that was done me when I was invited to take on the responsibility."

Across the table from Bill, Paddy Shaughnessy raised his eyes towards heaven.

"I had hoped that if any of you were unhappy about your work here, you would come to me first rather than make damaging allegations in the press."

"But I did come to you first," said Bill. "I came and complained when I found the protocol had been rewritten. You said you'd take it up with the executive and the next thing I knew was that the protocols had been sent out unaltered directly from your office."

"But if you'd only asked, dear boy, you would have learned that my best efforts in committee were, for once, in vain. Just because we are doctors we can't always get our own way. We have to accept these decisions, even when we don't approve of them. The alternative would be chaos and goodness knows there are too many examples of that around us in the world today."

"For Christ's sake, let's not forget what we're talking about," said Shaughnessy. "There's a ballsaching correspondence going on in the *Lancet* over whether there is or whether there isn't such a thing as informed consent, and Bill weighs in with a letter pointing out that in government departments the decision whether to obtain consent may not always be a medical one. Hardly the end of civilization as you and the colonel would like to know it."

"The point is, Shaughnessy, that it *was* a medical decision. In the final analysis, I am responsible and I'm happy to take that responsibility."

"Hold it there a moment," said Greg. "As I understand it, the original protocol was prepared by Bill and approved by you. Then it went to Security, only because every god-damned thing in this place goes to Security. And they removed the paragraph that insisted that only subjects who had given informed consent should be recruited."

"That's not strictly accurate," said Rex. "What happened was that Bill produced a draft which was sent around for comment before it was approved. Our colleagues in administration pointed out the controversy that existed over the business of informed consent and suggested that, as we were talking about a form of treatment which was quite extraordinarily complex in scientific terms, on this occasion the need for informed consent might be waived."

"Really?" said Greg. "I heard they were concerned that if too many people understood what they were getting, they might start wondering what we were up to."

Rex's cheeks reddened.

"Pure gossip," he said. "I refuse to discuss this important professional matter on the basis of canteen chit-chat."

Bill had been watching Kate. Her eyes were on the table as if embarrassed by the whole proceedings. Not once did she return his glance. Why was she always so bloody deferential to Rex? She had no problem being pointedly undeferential to everybody else.

Tim Craddock chipped in with fresh-faced earnestness.

"So Bill complained to you, sir. You took it up on the executive and you were overruled. Doesn't that mean that Bill's letter is right, sir, and the decision was not a medical one?"

Rex adopted a pitying tone.

"My dear boy, you may be a clever bacteriologist but your notion of the working of committees is remarkably naïve. Of course, we have full and frank discussions but, in the end, a consensus has to emerge. On this occasion, I fought our corner, saw I was outvoted, so went along reluctantly with the consensus. It didn't seem a matter of supreme importance. And my concession will not have gone unnoticed. It will weigh in our favour when we want to win some point more vital to our profession."

Bill couldn't take his eyes off Kate but she refused to raise her head. It was no good. He had to reach her. So he stood, crawled across the table, climbed on to her lap, and nestled his head between her breasts. Then, as she put her arms around him and kissed him gently on the forehead, the world came to a juddering halt.

Chapter Six

"Wakey, wakey," said the driver.

He'd already opened the door of the cab.

"Welcome to Woodall. I'm taking a thirty-minute break. Join me if you like. If you'd prefer an eyes-down in the cab, I'll have to lock you in."

"I'd like to get some sleep."

"Suit yourself."

The driver climbed from the cab, slammed the door shut, then locked it. Bill stretched himself across both seats and turned on his side. He was desperately tired but sleep seemed determined not to come. When he drifted into near-sleep, instead of oblivion there came images of Kate.

They were walking down the road towards the village having just gone through the security rigmarole at the gate.

"All very well for them," said Bill, "to tell us that the barbed wire, the security passes, and the closed-circuit TV are there to keep the animal liberationists out. I think they're there to keep our thoughts inside."

"You're beginning to be a bore," said Kate. "And paranoia is an infectious disease. It's antisocial of you to spread it around."

She bent and picked a pebble from the side of the road.

"Why can't you accept the world for what it is and take comfort wherever you can find it?"

She drew back her arm and flung the pebble far into the field beside them.

Two days later, after the row about his letter to the *Lancet*, he couldn't get to sleep and went outside. The moon was bright, the night still and soundless, even the animal houses were quiet, and the tracery of frost on the lawn crunched beneath his feet. As he passed one of the prefab huts that housed the chemical labs, he heard an odd, unclassifiable, yet unmistakably human sound.

He looked round a corner and there was Kate sitting on the steps outside the lab gazing at the ground in front of her. She saw his shadow and started. Then she recognized him. She stood and came towards him.

"What messenger summoned you?" she asked.

Both her cheeks glistened with tears.

"Only chance," he said.

"Thank you chance," she said. Then she put both arms on his shoulders and folded them around his neck.

"Hold me," she said.

She laid her head upon his shoulder and he held her gently, stroking her spine with his hands.

"This bloody place," she said. "It's destroying us all. Kiss me," she ordered.

And he did. First on her neck, then on her lips, then deep within her mouth.

Suddenly she pulled away and looked up at him with sparkling, mischievous eyes.

"Thank you, doctor," she said. "I feel much, much better."

And she was gone, running with awkward angular movements across the lawn towards the mess.

He closed his eyes and sought to re-embrace that warm, gently moving shape that had been in his arms, between his legs. But Security grabbed him, dragged him roughly away, shook him free.

"You really were away," said the driver. "Thought I'd have to throw a bucket of water over you."

He stood outside the open door of the cab and was leaning in, shaking Bill's shoulder.

"Sorry to disturb you, squire, but I'd like my seat back."

Bill sat up, massaging his face with the palms of both hands.

"Brought you a present," said the driver.

He handed Bill a T-shirt. Across its front was the slogan "I've been to Barnsley."

"Thought it might be handier than the pyjama top when you come in contact with civilization. And up here any friend of Barnsley is a friend of theirs."

Bill tried to pay him but was refused.

As the truck trundled out of the car park, Bill watched carefully in the mirror, and from his window, to see if anyone started up at the same time. They seemed to be the only people on the move as they drove slowly out of the park, past the fuel pumps, and down the slip-road.

Bill steadfastly refused to sleep. They passed the lights of Rotherham and then darkness. Somewhere out there was the village where he had spent his childhood and adolescence, but the coming of the motorway had changed the scale and he couldn't work out the relationship between the villages he knew and this broad highway. His sense of place was as disrupted as his more recent memory.

The driver had run out of conversation. He hummed a melody that Bill didn't recognize over and over again, sometimes slow, sometimes jerky, sometimes with passion, sometimes with angst. Then the steady rhythm of the diesel engine broke as they pulled off the motorway.

"We are now approaching Doncaster. Passengers should ensure they have all hand-baggage with them when they leave the truck. Anywhere special you'd like to be dropped? You have to be out before I reach the depot."

"Could I hang on till I see which way you go?"

"Fair enough, squire."

They crossed a bridge over the railway and a sign to their left saying "Carr Hill Industrial Estate", then rumbled along a road and round a roundabout that didn't seem familiar to Bill. Now they were passing rows of dark houses and he still didn't know where he was. He had lived here for the first eighteen years of his life and he couldn't recognize one yard of it.

Suddenly the shapes fell into place.

"Near the racecourse will do. If that's OK."

The driver looked up at the black sky.

"Don't fancy the visibility for the first race."

They pulled in opposite Doncaster Rovers football ground. Bellevue. Saturday afternoons with Dad when the Rovers were at home.

Bill climbed out, thanked the driver once again for the T-shirt and, on impulse, threw the Mark Phillips into the cab as a return gift. Only after the tail-lights had disappeared did he realize that handing over the cap had been a stupid mistake.

He crossed the open common to the racecourse. Away from the lights of the road, the sky looked less dark and the moonlight, filtering through a thin cover of haze, was enough to let him see where he was going as he followed the white rails round to his left. Soon he trod the very turf over which St Leger winners stretched towards the winning post. He looked at his watch: 2.15 a.m.

He turned towards the darkened stands and, in a corner of the grandstand terrace, found a pile of large plastic bags filled with waste paper. He dragged them into the angle of a wall, formed them up into a giant mattress, and clambered on top. Luxury. For a moment he lay on his back gazing at the overhang of the grandstand roof that protected him from the moonlight. Then he turned on his side and, within seconds, was asleep: no dreams, no memories, just blissful oblivion.

He woke to sunshine. His corner was in shadow but all around him the world had been lit as if for the filming of a musical. The grass was too green, the rails too white, the sky too blue. Maybe this enhanced perception of colour had something to do with breaking free; more likely it was to do with a low blood sugar.

He looked at his watch: 7.45. Then, as he tried to sit up, his colourful world receded. Each calf, each thigh, and a knot of muscles in his lower back, reminded him he was getting a bit old for gallivanting. The night in the clinic bed had set him back, dissipating the training his muscles had received the week before.

More worrying than the aching muscles were the sore feet. He'd slept, as a gentleman should, with his wellies on, and he didn't dare take them off now because he feared what he might find underneath. He tried a few tentative steps. Progress was painful but just possible. He took off the pyjama jacket, stuffed it in one of the plastic bags, and put on the T-shirt.

He tried to conjure up the figure he cut: T-shirt, pyjama trousers hidden with luck by riding mac and green wellies, one day's growth of beard. Best not thought about too closely. Yet once he'd crossed the first hundred yards of rough grass, his depression started to lift. His muscles loosened the way he hoped they would and even his feet reached some sort of accommodation with the forces that tormented them.

He reached the main road and, though it was still early morning, the sun was warm on his back. He passed Charlesworths' Garage where his dad had bought his last car, the Rockingham Arms which he was sure had been much grander when he'd gone there to a children's party, the park tennis courts where Miss Hepinstall had improved his backhand, the tall house where Mr Mullins had drilled his teeth.

And then, oh dear, he reached the Gaumont. For years the Gaumont's screen had been his only window on the world but now the temple had been sacked and degraded into three mini-cinemas. Vandals had been busy destroying his past while he was elsewhere trying to find his future.

He turned abruptly down the road towards the market and, as he did, his nose brought evidence that one memory had survived. The smell of frying still drifted up the hill from Len's Driver's Caff.

The counter had a covering of greasy check oilcloth and Bill ordered a bacon and egg sandwich and a cup of tea. He tried to use a neutral accent but he needn't have bothered. Nobody paid any attention. A scatter of men sat at tables or stood at the counter munching their breakfast, but each was engrossed in a newspaper. Even the man who served him paid him scant attention because he was in earnest dispute with a customer about what should or should not have happened to a horse which had run the day before at Haydock.

The hot food raised Bill's spirits to a level of euphoria that sustained him while he explored a monstrous Galleria which had been built down near the station. An Arndale shopping centre. He bought a pair of socks, a pair of sneakers, some cotton underwear, and a pair of jeans.

He used the Arndale's aromatic lavatory to put on these new clothes. His feet didn't look as bad as they had felt and the cotton socks and the soft leather of the sneakers gave snug support that acted like a balm. He left the green wellies on the top of the cistern. They would be a lucky find for any local collier with social aspirations.

Next he sought a shop which he hoped might still be where he'd last left it; it had a history of heroic endurance. Even during the war it had retained the title Army Surplus Store as though it dealt in bombs and rifles found to be in excess of His Majesty's requirements.

He found it exactly as he remembered it, windows still crammed with their traditional decorations: canvas tents, ruck-sacks, sheath-knives, boots, folding stools, torches, primus stoves, binoculars, waders, fishing-rods, footballs, even an occasional garden implement. Bill's only disappointment was that someone had changed the assistants during the past thirty years. The cunning old men, who could sell you not just one but half a dozen things you didn't need, had been replaced by brash youngsters who paraded their salesmanship more brazenly.

Bill took a look first at the rucksacks and anoraks, then at the boots, and confirmed that another tradition at the Surplus Store had not been subverted; though much of the stuff that cluttered the shop was tat, when it came to walking and fishing, life was taken seriously. It was a tradition that the old men would have been embarrassed to mention for fear it diminish their pride in their salesmanship.

He enjoyed the next half-hour. First he bought three pairs of long walking socks and two pairs of short. All were seamless with no ridges to rub against his skin.

With socks in place he approached the altar at which the central ceremony in the buying of walking gear takes place: the boot shelves. With the help of one of the young men, who put aside salesmanship in favour of the reverence demanded by the rubric, Bill tried on, laced up, and walked up and down in, half a dozen sorts of boot before choosing a pair of soft leather lightweights with Vibram soles.

He favoured the soft leather because it could be quickly "broken in" and the lightweights, as chosen, met the traditional demands: the boots' heels cupped his, the sides of his feet were firmly held not squeezed, the padded tongue and padded sides lay comfortably against his skin. Each boot had a scree cuff to grip the ankle and keep out small stones and, when he walked, he felt he'd been endowed with more satisfactory extensions to his legs than nature had provided.

He kept the boots on—"breaking in" couldn't start too soon—and moved away from the high altar. He spent less time choosing a dark-green anorak made of Gore-Tex and a rucksack which he proceeded to fill quickly and methodically: Gore-Tex trousers, two Viyella shirts, a woollen polo-neck, a small butane stove, a Swiss army knife, a mug, a large torch, a pair of binoculars, a Silva compass, a plastic map-case, a towel, and a groundsheet.

The young salesman, momentarily perturbed by the practicality of the sale, made a half-hearted attempt to encumber Bill with something called an Eatpak—chromium-plated knife, fork and spoon clipped to a thin plastic plate—if only to maintain his own and the shop's reputation, but Bill just smiled. When he paid in cash, the wad of notes grew depressingly thin.

He slipped the harness of the rucksack over his shoulders and, with his mac hanging incongruously over his arm, returned to the gentlemen's lavatory in the shopping centre. The cubicle he'd used before was empty and he was delighted to find the green wellies had already gone. He hoped they'd found a good home. Just in case their new owner came back to see if he'd missed anything, Bill put the mac on the top of the cistern. Only later did he realize that this was the third signal he had given that Bill Marsden had passed this way.

Before he left the shopping centre, he bought some canned food, a pack of disposable razors, an aerosol can of shaving foam, and a bar of soap. He also wandered into a stationer's and bought sheets 103 and 104 in the 1:50,000 Ordnance Survey series. It was an impulse purchase and, as he walked along Printing Office Street, he tried to work out why he had chosen those particular maps. He had a reason but it lurked just beyond the edge of retrievable memory.

The weight of the harness on his shoulders forced him to adopt a familiar upright stride. And with the stride came confidence. Happy this man who stepped out along the sunny pavement with his home on his back and a pair of good boots on his feet. Details he'd forgotten were beginning to return, seeping in under and over the barriers. Given time, all memory would return. Try to force it, and it would retreat.

When he reached Waterdale, he found that when the vandals rode into town they had also made off with the bus station. He wandered around for several puzzled minutes before asking the way of an old woman who lumbered arthritically by. She sent him back the way he'd just come and, as he thanked her, he grew aware of the incongruity of his request. Here he was, clad and accoutred for high peaks and empty valleys, yet looking for a bus that would take him to a colliery village he had last seen nearly twenty years before.

Yet somewhere within his malfunctioning brain lay the conviction that, at last, he was moving in the right direction.

Chapter Seven

He sat, as he had always sat, in the front seat on the top deck and when the bus turned off the Mexborough road he saw that the vandals had wrenched another symbol from the landscape. Gone was the pair of pit-head derricks whose spinning wheels announced each day that the pit was still alive. Only twice had he seen them stilled: once in 1941 the morning after a German bomber on its way to Sheffield unloaded its bombs seven miles short of its target, the second during a strike.

The winding gear was now hidden in a windowless box of battleship grey, its grotesque proportions diminishing the rows of back-to-back houses in the village. The pit could give no signal that it was dead. Yet dead it was, summarily executed as part of the victory celebrations after the miners' strike. Just retribution said those who'd read in their tabloids that Stannington Main supplied intransigent members of the Scargill praetorian guard.

He got off the bus at the pit gate, now just a gap in a brick wall with a desolate yard beyond it; no men leaning against the wall or squatting on their hunkers and pausing in their gossip to "How do?" the arrivals off the bus. He crossed the road and took a short cut across a barren patch of earth trodden so often that its top had been worn to underlying stone and buried bricks. Only the coarsest blades of grass had the strength to break through the packed surface. He passed the allotments— lots of activity there—and walked down a narrow lane that ran through the gap between two strings of terraced houses.

When he turned the corner into Wilberforce Street it looked for a moment as if it were decked out for a coronation or a royal wedding. The fronts of the houses, once uniform red brick, were hidden behind false façades of painted cement or mock stone reconstituted from dust or chippings. The colour of the paint ranged through the spectrum from red and orange to indigo and violet. And where once every window had been a uniform wood-framed sash, there was now an ill-assortment of plate-glass picture windows, aluminium frames, double-glazing as seen on television, bow-fronts with bull's-eye panes, and leaded lights which looked as ungenuine as the coach lamps screwed to the walls alongside them. The façades, the windows, and the lamps were declarations of status: symbols that the inhabitant now owned the house and was no longer restricted by the aesthetic choice of council or landlord.

The street was also festooned with bunting which, only to a second glance, revealed itself as gaudy signs erected by estate agents. Every sign seemed to say "For Sale"; Bill could see none that said "Sold". The new home-owning democrats were learning the market value of a house in a village whose only asset was a dead pit.

Bill climbed the sloping street to one of the few houses which retained a frontage of blackened red brick, and opened the gate through which he'd so often walked, and run, and skulked. Beyond the gate was the six-foot-deep "front garden" where neatly trimmed rose bushes lined two concrete paths. One led to the front door; the other, through a narrow passage alongside the house, to the backyard and the coal-house. Bill and his best friend Jimmy had once wheeled barrows of coal along that passage after Jimmy's dad, big John Embley, had shovelled them full from the load that the pit lorry had dumped in the road outside.

Bill stood on the familiar front step and faced the familiar green door. He slipped the rucksack from his back and gave a couple of sharp raps on the knocker. He must remember not to ask: "Can Jimmy come out now please?" Footsteps beyond the door, and then it was opened by a squat middle-aged woman wearing a plain blue apron over a floral dress.

She peered short-sightedly at Bill's face then her eyebrows shot up and her cheeks pulled back in a startled smile.

"You made it," she said.

Bill was puzzled.

"You expected me?"

"Of course."

"But why? It's over twenty years."

She looked at him thoughtfully.

"You're always expected here. Don't just stand there giving yourself varicose veins. Come inside."

She turned her head and shouted over her shoulder.

"Dad, have a guess who's here. It's young Jimmy's friend and he wonders why we're not expecting him."

She ushered Bill past her and, before she closed the door, went out on to the front step and looked carefully up and down the street.

The door led straight into the front parlour where the well-polished table and chairs stood, as they had always stood, as silent and unused as the upright piano in the corner. Here was one place which had stayed exactly as Bill remembered it. He crossed to the open door that led to the back room and there in the far corner, alongside the black-leaded kitchen grate, was a tall wooden chair padded with cushions. In the chair sat a big man, maybe eighteen stone, thin strands of hair, mostly jet black but a few grey, greased down to his skull, eyes alert above gold wire spectacles that sat askew near the end of his nose. He had looked up from the *Guardian* he'd been reading and was watching the door to the front room.

When he saw Bill he grabbed the walking-sticks that lay one each side of his chair and hauled himself up on to them. He had to lean on the sticks because his back bent forward from his hips at a sharp angle. His enforced stoop greatly reduced his height but the top of his head still seemed a good six feet above the ground. This massive man must now be in his eighties yet he looked the same as Bill always remembered him. He'd had his bent back since the day he'd been dug from a fall of coal that had buried him for twenty hours. He'd told the surgeon at Doncaster Infirmary, "Don't thee worry about me. Big lads like us spend all our time down't pit bent double," and this flawed giant had worked out his time on the coal-face until the osteoarthritis which is a miner's natural destiny had caught up with him.

He nodded his head solemnly at Bill.

"Good to see thee, lad. Brew us a couple of mugs of tea, Joyce."

"Watch it, Dad," said Joyce in the tones of a schoolteacher

67

reprimanding a favourite pupil. "I'll offer Bill some tea because he's a guest, and I'll get you some tea 'cos I promised to look after you. But I'll not brew tea because I'm ordered to. Now, Bill, would you like some tea?"

"Please," said Bill.

"That's all that bloody man Scargill has achieved," said the big man. "Given these women big ideas."

Then, as Joyce went out to the back kitchen, he subsided into his chair.

Bill sat where he always sat, in an upright chair alongside the scrubbed kitchen table.

Big John seemed puzzled. He stared at Bill as if expecting him to say something. The pause lengthened and was broken only by the noise of the tap as Joyce filled the kettle.

"Nothing to say then," said Big John.

A plop from the back kitchen as Joyce lit the gas.

"They came round asking about you so I said I hadn't seen you for mebbe twenty years."

"And they went away?"

"Don't worry, lad. They went away."

"I'm sorry we lost touch. It wasn't intentional. I always knew I'd come here one day."

"That's the way of the world, lad."

A rattle of crockery as Joyce took the cups from the cupboard.

"What's been happening to you, young Bill?"

"That's what I came to ask you. Somewhere in the back of my mind I know you've got part of the answer."

"That's a damn funny thing to say. I've heard you talk some riddles in your time, especially when our Jimmy were alive, so I suppose I shouldn't be surprised."

He carefully folded the newspaper that still lay across his lap and placed it on the floor beside him.

"You know that as your father's son you'll always be welcome in this house and if there's anything I can do to help you, you know I always will."

He had spoken without raising his eyes. Now he looked directly at Bill.

"There's just one thing I need to get clear. Before we start

68

talking about anything else, answer me one question. Is there a particular message you want to give me?"

He stared at Bill over those gold wire frames. Bill was puzzled. What was the big man after?

"I'm not sure what you're asking me."

John Embley waited for a moment then smiled.

"Fair enough," he said.

Then he raised his voice and bellowed: "Joyce. What's happened to that brew?"

Joyce popped her head round the scullery door.

"Andy Capp is alive and well and living in Wilberforce Street," she said.

She brought the tea not in mugs but in an aluminium teapot set on a tray with a jug of milk, cups and saucers, and a bowl of lump sugar with sugar-tongs. That was how her mother had served tea when young Bill, the doctor's son, came to play with young Jimmy. An uneasy silence hung between them while Joyce poured the tea, asked Bill if he still took sugar, and played out a social ritual that was a salute to people who were no longer present. She handed them their cups and took hers over to a wooden kitchen chair by the window.

They sipped their tea and the silence still hovered. Then the big man spoke.

"We were talking about your dad down at t'club t'other night." Again he gave Bill a questioning look as though inviting him to respond.

Bill just nodded.

"Glad he weren't around during the past two years. If he'd seen some of the things that happened here, he'd have wept. I wonder did you ever know what a hero your dad were in this village? He stood alongside us in the Thirties and I doubt we would ever have had pit-head baths if he hadn't put the fear of God into the colliery company. They used to say we wouldn't want baths and, if they did put them in, we wouldn't use them for fear we'd look soft. Them as lived in fancy houses knew that the likes of me preferred to walk home black with dust and sit in the middle of this room in a tub that Joyce's mother here topped up with kettles of water from the grate."

It was a story Bill had heard before. Young Bill in an itchy grey flannel shirt, short pants kept up with a snake-buckled belt, squatting on the hearth rug in front of that chair and looking up in wonder at the big man.

"That were just one of the things your dad did but people round here had another reason for worshipping him. He were always a kindly man."

Bill needed no reminder of what the village thought of his father. The day of his funeral, Bill and Marion had sat in the black limousine that had followed the hearse from Doncaster. As they rounded the corner from the Mexborough road they'd found the road blocked. Big John stood at its centre surrounded by miners in best suits. The big man stopped the hearse with an imperious gesture. The others opened the hearse, unloaded the coffin, and carried it on their shoulders through the streets, then along the steep uphill track that led to the cemetery.

The thronged cemetery had been noisy with gossip until the coffin appeared at the gates. Then the colliery brass band struck up "Abide with Me" and silence descended on the crowd until the second verse, when they all joined in with a vigour unmatched since the day Sheffield Wednesday got to the final at Wembley. Bill had watched Big John stand hatless and moist-eyed alongside the muddy hole in which he was about to lose his friend and wondered what his father had done to earn such love. Certainly not big things. They were celebrated with honours and decorations and commemorated by cathedral choirs. A bare-headed crowd, a brass band, and an honest declaration of love were earned by smaller things: an accumulation of small acts of sympathy and kindness, and occasional understanding, that the bestower rarely remembered because they were rarely offered consciously.

"Your dad would have stood with us this time too but he wouldn't have felt comfortable. This time were different. Before it started I used to get a lot of stick down the club by making mock of Scargill. And I still think Joe Gormley were a cannier man. But the young lads were all for Scargill and once the thing had started and he'd led us up shit creek, there was nowt to do but back him."

Joyce got up from her chair and put her half-full cup on the table.

70

"I'll just take another look out front," she said.

She went out through the front room and Bill heard her open the front door. He didn't hear her close it.

"I found it easier once those toffee-nosed buggers down south started smarming all over the telly. Then that woman sent up yobbos disguised as police. The Met. They ran amok in Askern and Armthorpe and I saw them clobbering young lasses down here by the pit gate. Your dad, like me, believed in the law but I reckon he'd find it as hard as me, and other decent folk round here, to believe those police had owt to do with law. Thatcher's storm troopers they called them here. And with good cause. When that lot arrived we knew we had to stick together. But I can tell you, there's not much fun sticking in a fight you know you've already lost."

Joyce came back and picked up her cup.

"Nowt much happening out there," she said, and went back to her chair by the window. The big man nodded at her then turned back to Bill.

"Ask anyone in this village now and they'll tell you Arthur was right. Maybe he was. Our number was up and young men prefer to go down with fists flying. The strike seems hardly over and the pit's already gone and half the shops down the road are boarded up. Walk down Wood Lane now and you'll find strong young men wheeling prams. Go next door and you'll find them watching last night's telly. Whatever else the strike did, it gave a boost to video machines. They switch 'em on in the evening and go down the club. Next day they sit indoors and watch all those programmes where you win a free knitting-machine for knowing who wrote *Hamlet*."

From somewhere beyond the backyard came children's voices raised in the rhythmic chant of a street game which dissolved occasionally into hysterical screams and laughter. The same chants, the same games, in the streets in which he'd played.

The big man pulled himself up from his chair and, moving at remarkable speed on his two sticks, crossed the room to the sideboard. He took out a tin of biscuits, prised off the lid, and waved the open tin at Bill. When Bill shook his head and said

"No thanks," the big man went back to his chair and, carefully selecting a fig roll, dunked it in his tea.

"Thank you for offering me one, Dad," said Joyce.

"You know you never take them, love."

He turned to Bill.

"The only people who've got anything out of this strike are the women. It's brought them out of the scullery and back to life. And a proper pain in the arse it's made some of them too."

He nodded at Joyce.

"But not all of them. The best thing to happen to her was when her man walked out on her. The next best thing was Arthur Scargill. The strike was the making of her. Big wheel in the support group. Cadging bags of spuds off grocery vans, then off to London for the first time ever. Fund raising. And now, do you mind, voluntary organizer with Women Against Pit Closures and a hotter political firebrand than her dad ever were."

Joyce was determined not to be drawn. She looked at the rucksack on the floor.

"Where are you off to, young Bill? You look as if you're about to climb Everest."

"Would you believe me if I said I didn't know?"

The awkwardness that had entered the room with him had long since disappeared.

"The big man always told me I could come here if I was in trouble."

John nodded.

"Well, I am in trouble, though I swear to God I can't tell you what it is. If I hadn't lived the past few days I doubt I would believe them."

John leaned forward.

"You don't have to tell us anything, lad, that you don't want to. If you tell us nowt, you're still welcome."

But Bill did want to tell them. So he told what he remembered of the treks by night, the hiding from the police, the walk with Ron through Dovedale, the chase, the fall. He told them about the clinic and how he got away, how he knew he had to keep moving, that there was something important he had to do, but he didn't know what or why.

Big John accepted the tale with no more incredulity than he showed each Saturday evening when he listened to the football results and checked his coupon.

"And you really can't remember owt about where you were heading?"

"I just have a crazy notion it had something to do with a fox but that fall disrupted my memory. Sometimes I half remember things in the way ideas can drift into your mind when you're sitting in the sun and you start to nod off. At first everything is logical, then it starts to get a bit illogical, then a bit more illogical, and then your head drops and wakes you up. And you just, but only just, can't remember what the first idea was."

"You don't have to sit in the sun for that, lad. Happens often enough in this chair. Too often these days for my liking."

"Sitting here," said Bill, "I feel I never left this place. Yet I did. And a lot has happened since I last saw you. You heard about Susie?"

"Aye, lad, we heard about that. And we were sorry. We heard she were a fine lass that your dad would have been proud of. Don't ask me how we knew she'd passed on. But we all did. This village keeps tabs on its own."

"We'd have written if we'd known where you were," said Joyce.

Bill felt a sudden shame that the thought of writing to them had never entered his mind.

He started to talk again and words came easily. How long had it been since he last talked to people whom he could trust?

He tried to explain how happy the last two years with Susie had been. Because they knew the sentence that hung over her they had no time for pretence. Her illness made him realize that he too suffered from a fatal disease called mortality and, for two years, they both lived at a breathless intensity, always aware that the days they had left on this earth were ticking away, finding wonder in the world because they were doing, or seeing, or hearing things not for the first time but maybe for the last.

"We weren't morbid. For most of the time we were happier than we'd ever been before. It's the nearest I've ever come to living without anxiety."

73

"Did she suffer much pain?" asked Joyce. "Were there nothing they could do?"

No pain, said Bill. And yes everything had been done.

"You were fortunate," said the big man. "I never had any time like that with our Jimmy. That's what I hate about the way he were taken. Useless. Riding a trials bike up and down a hill all afternoon without so much as a spill. Then one skid on a wet road on the way home. What a bloody waste."

Joyce looked at him anxiously. She turned quickly to Bill.

"Are you stopping here for a few days, young Bill?"

"Course he is," said the old man.

"Well I'd best make up a bed. I don't live here you know. I'm two doors down but I pop in for an hour each day to make sure the old bugger's behaving himself. You look as though you could do with some hot food inside you. There's enough in the fridge to do you a fry-up."

She turned to her father.

"I suppose you'll want one too."

"Can a duck swim?" asked the old man.

She collected the empty cups, put them on the tray, and carried them out to the back kitchen.

"She's a good lass," said the big man. "Let's leave any more talking till you've got some food inside you. You were always a long thin streak. Your dad never could get any meat on your bones."

He picked up the newspaper from the floor and held it out to Bill.

"Have a look at this and see if you can find any sense in it."

Bill got up and took the paper. The old man leaned back against his cushions and closed his eyes. Within a minute he was snoring. Bill tried to read but his eyes kept wandering around the room recapturing events that had happened here. From the back kitchen came the splutter of hot fat and the smell of frying bacon. Then Joyce appeared with a crisp checked cloth and Bill got up to help her. She went back to the kitchen and reappeared with a tray bearing two large plates laden with fried eggs, bacon, fried bread, and black pudding, a bread board on which rested a home baked loaf, and two large mugs of dark tea. She laid two places.

74

"Dad," she called loudly and the old man woke with a snort.

"Surprised I had to wake him," she said. "Smell of food usually brings him round like smelling salts."

Then she disappeared upstairs and the two men settled at the table.

Bill attacked his plate eagerly. He was indeed hungry and he ate voraciously and with barely a pause.

Joyce came downstairs. "Bed's made," she said. "I'll be off now, Dad. I've got to do that job we were talking about. I'll take the car."

Her father looked puzzled. Then he glanced up at her.

"Oh, of course," he said. "You do that, love. When shall we see you again?"

"I'll look in in't morning."

When they finished, Bill carried the crocks into the back kitchen. The old man returned to his chair and, before he sat down, put a couple of shovels of coal into the grate from the scuttle that stood alongside it. Bill washed up the plates and cutlery and left them to dry on the draining-board. When he came out of the kitchen, the big man told him to pull his chair over to the grate.

Then, while Big John sat propped against his cushions, gold wire glasses now pushed back to the bridge of his nose, Bill started to talk and found the words flowed out of him. No digging at memory now, he just told things as they'd happened.

"When Susie died most of the energy that had kept us going seemed to die with her. I sold the house too quickly and only after it had gone I realized I hadn't sold unpleasant memories but happy ones. Then, out of the blue, I was offered a new job and I thought it might help. At St Thomas's, I'd still been seeing patients every day but had spent a lot of my time mapping out the patterns of disease to see if the patterns gave any clue to the causes. Its called epidemiology and, now I've told you, you know more than at least one government minister."

Big John frowned. Bill didn't bother to explain.

"One day an old chum rang and said why didn't I apply for a job that had come up at St Christopher's where they were setting up a new department and were looking for someone to help organize tests on drugs—mainly new drugs but an occasional old one. Department of Clinical Pharmacology it was called.

"They were keen to try new ways of organizing tests and my chum thought I was the sort of chap they were looking for. So I applied and found the job would involve a lot of travelling round the country which seemed no bad thing. Anything that got me out of the depressing flat I'd rented in Islington would have been a good idea."

He paused, suddenly noticing that the eyes that watched him from beyond the wire-framed spectacles were untouched by time. The same alert eyes that had signalled interest in his childhood prattle egged him on now.

"I showed the right amount of enthusiasm at the interview and got the job. New drugs get tested first in healthy people, usually the testers themselves, and later in volunteer patients. I dealt with drugs that had passed all the early tests and were ready to be tried in patients to see how well they worked. A single hospital may see too few people suffering from some diseases to get a true idea of how well a drug works against them. I set up tests that could be done under the same conditions at different hospitals. That way, though we might get only a few volunteer patients at each, when we added the results together we had a decent measure of the drug's effects, good and bad.

"I didn't do any of the actual testing myself; doctors already working at each hospital did that. I had to make sure they all did it under the same conditions. I still saw a few patients at St Christopher's and taught students on two mornings a week, but I had to spend a fair amount of time in an office drawing up plans of treatment, keeping in touch with the doctors doing the tests and the drug companies who made the drugs, and trying to interpret figures that kept spewing out of the department's computer. But I also had to visit each centre, checking the way the tests were being done and enthusing the testers. That meant I spent more nights in hotels and fewer in that depressing flat in Islington."

"Do you know," said Big John, "that in all my days, I've never spent a night in a hotel. And that's God's truth. When the kids were young, we always took us holiday, if we got one, in a guest-house in Skegness. And when Joyce and I go to Blackpool now we do the same. The only time I've been abroad was a day trip to the Isle of Man."

Bill had a feeling he was being teased.

"I don't know that you missed much," he said. "At the start, all the trials we set up were here in Britain but in the late 1970s and early '80s, before people realized that the money this country was prepared to spend on health was about to run out, there'd been a great passion for setting up huge trials using hospitals in different countries. And I suppose because our department was new, and I was available, we soon got involved in those as well. Then I found myself visiting hospitals in Europe or taking part in meetings abroad organized by drug companies or by people like WHO, the World Health Organization.

"A couple of years ago I was in Copenhagen on a WHO working party when this rather grand doctor Rex Copeland— Sir Rex to you, Big John—asked if I'd like to join a team he was putting together for a special project.

"He got the timing exactly right. Our department at St Christopher's was bound to suffer in the cuts and Rex made the job sound interesting. I wouldn't have to leave the staff at St Christopher's; I would just be on loan for three years, which meant I wasn't cutting all connection with the past. And because Sir Rex's unit was in Cheshire I'd have a more honest way of escaping from London than dashing off to identikit rooms in identikit hotels.

"So I took the job. It was an odd sort of project bcause what we were testing wasn't really a drug at all, more a sort of vaccine that had been around for nearly thirty years and which we knew was safe. For years people had suggested it might be a successful treatment for cancer but they'd never been able to find out if it was because nobody could make enough of the stuff to test it properly.

"Then the people working with Sir Rex found a way of making it in large quantities and he wanted me to organize the hospital tests. The tests went well. We had no problems with safety and, when the first results came in, I can remember us all getting very excited."

His voice tailed off.

"And then something went wrong, terribly, catastrophically wrong. Nothing to do with the stuff we were testing. That was a great success. Nothing to do with me. I'm certain of that. Something else . . ."

Bill was staring, unseeing, at the dull glow in the grate. He looked up at the big man.

". . . but I have not the slightest notion what it was."

John Embley leaned forward as if to prompt Bill. Then he seemed to think better of it and leaned back against his cushions.

The room was dark and Bill noticed for the first time that, beyond the lace curtains, squalls of rain were lashing against the window.

The big man leaned forward again.

"You made a good run at that lad. One more stride and you'd have made it. Happen it'll not take long before it all comes back."

That afternoon, a cold wind from the north lashed the rain across the slates of the terraced houses and the sky assumed the aspect of a winter's day. In the back room at Number 34 the two men sat alongside the glowing grate and, while Bill talked and joked about the past with Big John, the tension eased out of him.

Later he raided the fridge in the back kitchen and found some cold ham and salad for their tea. This time the old man helped with the washing-up and then settled himself in front of the television set that stood on a wobbly table in the corner. He sat very close to it, peering intently at the screen over the top of his spectacles, and talking back angrily at a government minister who turned up on the early evening news preaching the virtues of pay restraint.

"Then why did you vote yourselves an extra sixteen per cent, you big ha'porth? And how about your friends in the City? One of them just gave hisself one hundred and three per cent, and he had a damned sight more than the likes of us before he started. Now give us a chorus of 'Nearer My God to Thee'."

78

The big man was a participating viewer. The news got a lot of talk back.

"Are you trying to tell me, John Humphrys, that they haven't stitched up John Stalker?"

And so did the quiz show that followed.

"If you can't answer that, missus, they should never have paid your bloody fare."

Bill watched for a while but weariness had enwrapped him and, with apologies to John, he decided on an early bed. He opened what he'd always thought of as the cupboard door leading to the stairs. Those stairs had intrigued him as a child because, thanks to the thin partition that separated them from the back room, they seemed to be hidden in a wall.

He washed at the basin in the tiny bathroom John had built over the back kitchen and, with a guilty feeling that he was giving himself a self-indulgent treat, put on another set of the clean underwear he had bought that morning in Doncaster.

The sheets were refreshingly cool against his skin and the soft mattress seemed not just to cushion but to caress his aching muscles. He lay on his back. Sodium light from a lamp down the street produced a shadow play on the ceiling as the curtains billowed with each gust of wind. This had been Jimmy's room and he wondered how many times his friend had watched the same patterns.

He heard voices downstairs. One, he was sure, was Joyce's. Then the front door slammed and the house was silent.

Outside, the world was cold and wet and troubled; in this room he was warm and content. Maybe if he concentrated hard enough, the world would stop, rewind forty years, and start all over again: Jimmy asleep in his bed, Big John and his dad drinking beer down at the Welfare, Bill tucked up in his own bed in the stone house at the foot of the hill, and an unknown future, exciting and unpredictable, lying ahead of them all . . .

Within a few minutes he had sunk into a deep and untroubled sleep.

Outside, the juggernauts were lined up under the floodlights. The police escort had already arrived and a sergeant was directing the cars into position.

Inside, the man in the black running vest sat on his own at a table in the canteen, facing the window, clutching a mug of tea in both hands, and watching the manoeuvring police and the bustle around the loading bays.

A young man came up and smacked him on the shoulder.

"What happened to you last night, Terry?"

The man in the black vest looked up.

"What do you mean, what happened to me?"

The young man sat opposite him.

"Just after we'd gone by the M6, I saw you up ahead. I'd about caught up when you turned off. I gave you a flash."

"So that was you. Might have guessed."

"Suddenly taken short were we? Must have been urgent. There was a service pull up ahead. You should see a doctor. Could need a rebore."

"What a clever little bugger you are. If you must know I was on to a bit of free-lance last night."

"Is that what they call it now?"

"Oh, piss off."

The man in the black vest took a swig of tea from his mug.

"A nice little earner, if you prefer. And a pleasant change from that bloody motorway. A little bit of taxi-ing, some gentlemanly conversation, and a comfortable feeling in the wallet."

He patted the hip pocket of his jeans.

"Nice people. Cash in hand. No questions. Ready to fix me a story if I couldn't make up time."

Another swig from his mug.

"They didn't have to bother. Had to wait less than thirty minutes before they set me on the job. Even had time for a stop at Woodall."

"Are you having me on, Terry?"

Terry smiled and shook his head.

"Who set you up for that then?"

The man in the black vest finished his tea and stood.

"Now, wouldn't you like to know?"

Chapter Eight

He came round as if from an anaesthetic, with no sense that time had passed. He had closed his eyes and then reopened them and, in that blink, the world had moved twelve hours forward. The curtains had been drawn back, bright yet ungolden sunshine filled the room, and a shadow hovered over him. As his eyes struggled to refocus, the shadow resolved itself into Big John.

"You were well away then," he said. "I never thought I'd get you to wake. You'd best take a look at this. Joyce brought it round."

He pushed a tabloid paper into the range of Bill's refocusing vision. The first thing his eyes registered was the headline: "Top boffin missing"; the next was the photograph beneath. He was looking at himself in a mirror: himself as he had been before he shaved away his beard.

A black box labelled the story "Exclusive".

Mystery last night surrounded the disappearance of a top scientist from one of Britain's cloak-and-dagger research centres.

Dr William Marsden, 52, walked out of his secret laboratory in north-west England two weeks ago and has not been seen since. He took no personal possessions and his colleagues are said to be puzzled.

Sources close to the Ministry of Defence confirmed last night that Dr Marsden, who is a medical doctor, was working on a top secret defence project and is an expert in biological warfare.

Security forces have mounted an intensive undercover man-hunt and Ministry spokesmen admitted yesterday that ports and airports were being watched.

Before joining the secret project, Dr Marsden was a top specialist at St Christopher's Hospital in London.

A hospital spokesman said last night that the missing doctor was an international expert on drug safety but had not been seen at the hospital since joining the government project two years ago. Dr Marsden is a widower and has no children. His wife, also a doctor at St Christopher's, died five years ago.   .

Tory MP Peter Bruinvels called last night for an immediate investigation into the security screening of scientists who work on projects of vital importance to the nation.

How safe are the nation's secrets? See Page 7.

The headline was the secondary one on the page. The big black type had been reserved for "Di Twists Ankle".

Big John gave him an encouraging grin.

"How's it feel to be a top doctor?" he asked. "Reckon it's more interesting than being a bottom one."

Bill was more angry than frightened. Mysterious disappearance, secret research? Two nights before he'd had a civilized conversation with his boss and his work was so secret that hundreds of doctors did it every day. And the only biological warfare in which he'd engaged was blasting bacteria with antibiotics.

The big man tried to defuse the anger. He got Bill to shave and dress, and kept off the subject of the newspaper story until they'd both eaten the toast he'd made. Then as they sat at the table in the back room drinking tea from large mugs he picked the newspaper from the chair and put it on the table between them.

"Whatever it is you've forgotten, lad, it isn't just the tea lady's phone number."

"How can they get lies like that into the paper?"

"Don't ask that in this village. They'll wonder where you've been for the past two years. More important is what we're going to do about it. First thing I must do is come clean about something we didn't tell you yesterday. Reckoned you'd had enough then and I were going to tell you this morning. There's been some odd fish hanging round the village the past week. Three of them.

"It's not easy to hide yourself in this place. Strangers are as out of place here as bowler hats and umbrellas. These three have tried to make out they're some kind of reporters or researchers. But we saw plenty of that sort during the strike and according to what I've been told these three don't match up. I won't ask you to guess who I think they are. The point is that they haven't called at this house yet. But I wonder how long it will be before they do? Now they've printed that . . ."

He tapped the newspaper.

". . . they can go where they like and say who they are, and expect to get answers."

"There's only one thing for me to do. I'll get out of here this morning. I don't want to drag you into this."

"Don't talk daft. If you walk out of here now you're as good as walking straight into their arms. You listen to me. I've had time to think this out while you were asleep. If we did get you out of here, where would you go?"

Bill shrugged.

"I'm sure I could think of somewhere. It was only instinct that led me here. It'll lead me somewhere else. Meanwhile I could hide up in Stannington Woods."

"By Christ, you have no more sense now than you had as a kid. Stannington Woods these days has so many lads on't dole walking whippets and kids, you'd find it easier to hide in the middle of Doncaster market. Joyce and I have had a long talk and we've decided there's only one place for you to go."

"And where's that?"

"Marion's."

"Marion's!" Bill's rising inflection expressed his disbelief. "I haven't seen Marion since my father died. It must be over ten years since we even sent Christmas cards. It's not that we don't get on. We just went our different ways. And, apart from anything else, I'm not sure where she's living now."

"She's still in the same place. That's why it's a good place to go. But it's also a bit of a problem. Where she lives, I mean. Getting you out of here will be a picnic compared with getting you in there. But Joyce and I reckon we've sorted a way of doing both. It'll not be easy but when you meet Marion you'll find out why going there is such a bloody good idea."

"You're enjoying talking in riddles, aren't you?"

The big man chuckled.

"You're right, you know. But remember the only excitement I get these days is shouting at the bloody telly."

He looked at the alarm clock on the mantelpiece.

"I promise I'll explain but first hang on a sec."

He switched on the old wireless set that stood on a shelf beside his chair. It was already tuned to Radio 4 and crackled to life just as the news summary began. The disappearing scientist was item number three. The Minister of Defence had refused to comment on newspaper speculation that Dr Marsden had worked on biological weapons but did confirm that he was missing and that inquiries were being made into his whereabouts. This time he had priority over Di. Her ankle was reported to be getting better.

That was just the first of the news bulletins they listened to; they tried to catch every one on mainline BBC and on local radio. By *The World at One*, Bill had become the leading item: no new lies but a lot more speculation and, in a pair of follow-up interviews, Robin Day spoke to an admiral who thought defence cuts were endangering national security and an adenoidal spokesman for PAB, People Against Biological Warfare. Sir Robin purred at the navy and growled at the adenoids.

In between the radio listening, the big man outlined the plans that Joyce and he had concocted and, with one or two changes, they won Bill's approval.

The sky was grey and overcast but it wasn't raining and the air was heavy and warm, so it seemed quite natural for the big man to spend near an hour, mid-morning, leaning on his sticks by his front gate, gossiping with anyone who went by. When he came back he announced he'd had no reports of strangers hanging round in the street, not that he'd expect them to be that stupid. More important, he'd heard no gossip about unusual happenings in the village.

Joyce came round midway through *The World at One* to cook them some dinner and, this time, she allowed Bill to give her a hand.

She'd already set up what she needed for her part of the plan. After dinner the three of them sat round the table in the back room. Joyce had brought two maps—Bill didn't like to tell her he already had one of them in his rucksack—and together they traced out the route he would have to follow.

The afternoon dragged on as though the hands on the mantelpiece clock were immersed in oil. On the news bulletins, Bill started to slip down the batting order; no one, it seemed, had been able to screw more information out of the Ministry of Defence.

The big man and Bill cooked themselves an enormous tea and Bill ate most of what they produced, devouring it with the dedication of a man who's not at all sure where his next meal is coming from.

The evening seemed to stretch to near infinity. They could do nothing until it grew dark and Bill discovered that a watched sky never darkens. Then, just as he resigned himself to at least another fifteen minutes of inaction, things started to happen. There was a rat-a-ta-tat on the front-door knocker and Bill hid on the staircase while Embley went to answer it. On the doorstep stood a boy aged about eight. As soon as the door opened, he rushed breathlessly into the message he'd been repeating to himself all the way up Wilberforce Street.

"Mr Embley, Mrs Next Door says could you please ask your Joyce whether she need bring any milk with her when she comes to t'next meeting and that's all there is to it bye."

He produced a sunburst of a smile, spun on his heel and went hoppity skip through the gate and down the street.

Big John closed the door and returned to the back room.

"Time to go, lad," he said.

Bill came down from the stairs and realized with shame that through all that long afternoon and evening he'd never got round to thanking the big man for what he'd done. There was so much he wanted to say and now there was no time. He put his arms around that massive neck, laid his cheek against Big John's and they stood for a moment in a silent embrace.

"Look after thee-sen, lad," said the big man.

Bill's rucksack lay in a corner. He picked it up and went through the kitchen, out the door, and across the yard to the back gate, ducking instinctively under a clothes-line that was no longer there. He paused alongside the coal-house that had once been the outside lavatory and opened the wooden gate. The big man had drawn the bolts earlier that evening and it swung back noiselessly. Beyond, a narrow alley ran left and right, separating the wall that backed the ribbon of houses of Wilberforce Street from the wall that backed the identical ribbon of Victoria Street.

Bill didn't look out, just stood in the gateway. No sound came from the alley. Then he heard footsteps, light footsteps swift and irregular, coming down the alley on his right. The steps grew louder and into view came the same small boy. He stopped outside the gate and looked up at Bill.

"Ay up, mister," he said. "Mrs Next Door says could you please ask your Joyce whether she need bring any milk with her when she comes to t'next meeting and that's all there is to it bye."

And off he went down the alley to Bill's left. Bill allowed him to go twenty yards, then followed. He knew that if the boy met anyone in the alley he would come back and warn him. After some eighty yards the alley took a right-angled turn towards Victoria Street and, as Bill rounded the corner, he saw the boy waiting where the alley opened into the street. He waited until Bill came up to him then skipped away.

The opening to the alley was in shadow and Bill took a couple of steps out on to the pavement and looked up and down the ill-lit street. It seemed deserted but, even as he looked, the loom of a car's headlights came round the corner down the street to his left. He stepped back into the alley.

The car—or was it a lorry, the engine sounded too heavy for a car?—came slowly up the street and stopped outside the alley. It was neither car nor lorry but a battered van and it had parked just three yards from where Bill stood motionless in the shadows. The engine was switched off but no one got out. Bill could see the driver, broad-shouldered and wearing a dark cap. The van just stood there. Silent. Bill began to grow edgy and then the driver restarted the engine. At that signal, Bill dashed round the back of the van, opened one of the doors, threw in his rucksack, and flung himself after it. He barely had time to close the door before the van moved off.

He squatted on the floor amid cardboard cartons. The shape of the driver was outlined against the windscreen and, as the van rounded the corner out of Victoria Street and rattled down Queen's Crescent towards the pit gate, the silhouetted head half turned towards him.

"Sorry I was a bit late," said the driver. "A couple of folk I didn't recognize walked across the foot of Victoria Street and I thought I'd best give 'em time to clear out of the road."

The voice was Joyce's. Her shape was bulked out by an old army greatcoat, the cap was her father's, and Bill was aboard the only capital asset of Stannington Women Against Pit Closures.

Chapter Nine

Bill sat on the floor in the back of the van. He'd wanted to sit up front but Joyce wouldn't let him. She had good reason, the same reason why they were going to keep clear of motorways and why she was going to get rid of this daft cap and this stifling greatcoat once they'd cleared the village. She didn't want to be identified too easily before they left but once they were away from Stannington, a van occupied by one driver, and that a woman, was less likely to be stopped by the police. Something she'd learned the hard way during the strike, and since.

Bill suspected that just three years ago this squat, middle-aged woman had been living out the future that her mother would have wished for her "plain Jane" daughter: a respectable woman who knew her place, who accepted commiserations because she hadn't any children, and was known as a "treasure" who looked after her dad and helped out with the old folk in the street. A woman who kept her unhappiness to herself and the doctor who gave her pills for it.

But then her mother would never have guessed that her quiet, law-abiding daughter would be locked up for a night in a police cell for protesting to a sergeant and his mate who were beating up a sixteen-year-old lad outside her gate, or that she would stand in a dock and earn sanctimonious rebuke and a heavy fine for "assaulting" the police. Joyce Embley had had an intensive course in the street wisdom of the Eighties.

That afternoon it had not been the big man but a track-suited Joyce who had briefed Bill on the plans she had made for his exit from Stannington, who had recruited the young lad next door and got him to play the game she'd taught his big brother to play in the strike, who had, like a schoolteacher, got Bill twice to repeat the details of the next stage of his trip, had checked his rucksack and changed some of the contents, and had insisted that, from the moment they left the house, they must always assume they were being followed even though they saw no sign of followers.

And it was Joyce who now sternly drove him through the night. She spoke only when they passed through a village or town, saying naught else but its name. The litany catalogued Bill's past. First came places he once rode through on his bicycle: Sprotbrough, High Melton, Barnburgh, Goldthorpe, Darfield. Later would come places he had driven through with his dad, usually on the way to a football match: Staincross, Ossett, Batley, Gomersal, Cleckheaton.

By the time they'd reached the fringe of bicycle territory Bill was none too comfortable. He had rested his back against one of the cardboard cartons and drawn his knees up to his chest, but the only insulation between his bottom and the metal floor was an uneven carpet of loose paper that had spilled from the boxes he'd knocked over when he jumped in. In her one conversational moment, when she triumphantly announced they had cleared the village on the back road and there was no sign of them being followed, Joyce had told him he was sitting on subversive leaflets produced by the "Enemy Within".

Another phrase of the Eighties, a wartime favourite making a comeback. Anyone who isn't one of us is an enemy. A frequent question of the colonel in charge of security. Is he one of us?

On that first day at the Centre, when they were all chattering in the canteen, the colonel had appeared behind Kate and tapped two pudgy fingers on her shoulder.

"I hear you've been ruffling the feathers of some of my chickens, Miss Hutchison," he said.

"Dr Hutchison to you," said Kate. "And I can't remember ever seeing a chicken with unruffled feathers. I've made my complaint to Sir Rex so you'll have to deal with him."

Tim Craddock, whose response to any inflammatory remark was to rush in like a fireman, leaped to his feet to introduce Bill. The colonel shook Bill's hand with a vigour that contrasted with his sleepy expression. Then he dragged over a chair from another table.

"Trained at Tommy's, didn't you? One of the best. Had a cousin there. Bit before your time. Johnny Costelloe?"

"I know *of* him, of course," said Bill.

But then everybody knew *of* Sir John Costelloe, the Rollo Suavely of private practice, who had astutely spurned Harley Street in favour of Eaton Square and earned a knighthood for services to the rich.

The colonel didn't dwell on the matter. Johnny the cousin was a credential establishing that he and Bill were members of the same club—the "one of us".

"Welcome aboard. Good crowd here. Hand-picked. Other places like to call themselves centres of excellence, we take the phrase literally and spend a lot of time and money making sure we are one. It may hearten you to know, my boy, that we screened over two hundred names before we even approached you. We reckon we've got the right chap for the job."

"Congratulations," said Shaughnessy. "You're now front-runner for *The Guinness Book of Records*. The bullshit when I was hired was that I was picked from a hundred and fifty."

"Scoured all of East Brisbane for me," said Greg Wilkinson.

"And I was the best out of one," said Kate. "But then I am a woman."

The colonel sat silent and apparently asleep while the others spoke. It was bullshit, thought Bill, and low-quality bullshit at that, yet he couldn't deny that a venal corner of his brain had responded to the flattery. Man *was* a venal creature and these army folk were good pragmatic psychologists. That's why they led men off to die to the sound of music.

The colonel half opened his eyes.

"I hear you've had a grand tour with one of my lords and masters. What do you think of our little venture?"

"Very impressed," said Bill politely. "But a bit like Fort Knox. Those steel gates in the front hall give the National Trust image a bit of a knock and those television cameras scanning the park must be a deterrent to young lovers."

"Animal liberationists have a lot to answer for," said the colonel. "Every research institution in the country has to mount this sort of security now. Damned shame. Waste of scarce resources. Absolute mayhem if they got in. Got to keep them out somehow."

And Bill Marsden sitting on, photocopied subversion in the

back of a van approaching Barnsley remembered the analogy. A medical congress in Berlin and they'd all been taken through Checkpoint Charlie for a peep behind the curtain. After a tour of the carefully nurtured exhibits of East Berlin, he'd asked the gaunt woman who was their guide the only question he wanted answered.

"Anyone visiting this city can't help wondering why, if it is as marvellous as you say it is, you had to build a wall around it to keep the people in."

The guide smiled a reassuring smile and gave him response number four from the handbook.

"Workers in the other zones in the city have discovered the social benefits we make available to our workers. If we did not control their entry from the West, we would be inundated."

He couldn't let her get away with that.

"Are you trying to tell us that, after all we've seen today, the layout of the mines and tripwires, that the wall exists to keep West Berliners out and not East Berliners in?"

She treated the question with imperious disdain.

"Of course," she said.

Joyce had been silent for a long time. The sky was cloudless, the moon was bright and, beyond the windscreen, the old West Riding was built of silhouettes. Tall chimneys rose beside empty mills and half-demolished factories, cathedral ruins of the industrial revolution.

"Hold tight," said Joyce.

She slammed on the brakes and brought the van to a shuddering halt before backing it slowly off the main road. She switched off the engine and came round and opened one of the back doors. They were parked in front of rusty factory gates secured by chain and padlock to protect a vast expanse of concrete yard ravaged by weed and thistle and scattered with bricks.

Joyce held a small transistor radio. Earlier she'd tried to listen to it while they were on the move but all they'd heard was electronic crackling. Now she sat on the floor of the van alongside Bill and switched it on. A serenade young Mozart had written as background music for a party in Vienna came through as clearly as if they were in the gardens of the Schönbrunn Palace. They listened in silence to the last few minutes of the music. Then came the news. Bill was still in the middle order of the batting. Sightings had come in from all over the place. The police claimed to be following them all. They were also said to be examining evidence that he may have been in the Doncaster area. Bill hoped that didn't mean the green wellies had been taken into custody. A police spokesman had no reason to believe that Dr Marsden had left the country.

Joyce switched off the radio. "Don't like that bit about Doncaster," she said. "They could all have the number of this van in their notebooks by now. Makes it all the more important we stick exactly to the plan. Still happy about that?"

Bill nodded assent.

"Keep your head down while we get through Keighley. Then I'll take the Skipton bypass."

She closed the van door, climbed back into the driver's seat, restarted the engine, and pulled out into the road. Bill tried to build a cushion of leaflets between his aching bottom and the vibrating metal floor. Then he leaned back against a carton and tried to doze off. Unsuccessfully.

"Gisburn," intoned Joyce.

Ten minutes silence, then Joyce spoke again.

"There's lots of traffic on this road. I expected lorries but there's cars and caravans as well. You'd have thought caravans would have settled down somewhere for the night by now. Must be on their way to the motorway. No choice now. We'll have to do it as we planned. I reckon it'll be another ten minutes but I'll give you plenty of warning."

Now that Bill needed to stay awake, he started to nod off. Sod's law.

Ten minutes passed. Fifteen. Then Joyce spoke.

"Just passed the sign at the top of the hill. I'll slow down to let this lorry past then you'll feel us going downhill."

A roof-rack lashing, a short band of elastic rubber with a metal hook at each end, was looped round a hook on the side of the van. Bill unravelled it, hooked one end to a bolt near the top of the nearside door, stretched the lashing, and hooked the other end to a strut in the roof. Then he turned the handle of the door to open the bolts. He pressed with both hands against the door and it opened slightly. When he eased the pressure, the elastic lashing snapped the door closed.

"Door's ready," he said.

"That lorry's gone past," said Joyce. "But there're still lights behind us. Looks like a car. I doubt they'll be close by t'foot of hill. Won't be long now."

Bill knelt facing the van doors. His right hand gripped the harness of his rucksack; his left an old walking-stick the big man had given him. The van slowed and swung to the left.

"Now," shouted Joyce.

Bill flung himself at the door and, as it yielded in front of him, tried to roll to his right. Joyce had let the nearside wheels drift over the grass verge and that's where he landed. The ground was soft and he thumped on to it so gently he didn't even catch his breath.

He lay still. The lights of the car that had been behind them were still a long way off and he lay almost in the entrance to a driveway. The rubber lashing had snapped the van door closed behind him and the van's lights already seemed far away, their brightness rapidly diminishing as Joyce sped on. Even a close observer would have seen no more than the van slowing momentarily to take a sharp corner, as it had slowed at every sharp corner since Stannington, and then accelerating away.

Anyone who cared to follow it would have to visit Blackpool, drive once along the front, and, after watching the van being refuelled, follow it home along a more elaborate route through the centre of Manchester and across old moorland roads to Sheffield.

Bill stood in the driveway, hidden from the road by a neatly trimmed hedge. Three cars passed—it was too dark to see if they contained passengers—then a couple of rumbling lorries. His eyes accommodated to the change of light. The cloud seemed to be building up but there was still some moonlight, enough to find his way by, and off to his left was a bright loom of light. Behind him was the unmistakable outline of Pendle, the massive fell that dominated the Ribble valley.

He waited till the road was clear, then scuttled across,

climbed a low fence and scrambled down a grass slope to the bank of Swanside Beck, a tributary of the Ribble.

The moonlight was a godsend and the river made navigation easy. He just had to follow it. His cramped muscles enjoyed the freedom to flex themselves again and the sound of the river running across stones helped clear his mind of anxiety.

When he reached the Ribble, it led him round the back of Chatburn and, as he followed it towards the next village, Grindleton, he saw that the glow in the sky, now helping him as much as the moonlight, came from some sort of factory along the valley. At its centre was a high tower festooned with blazing lights.

Near Grindleton the river ran close to a road, and he had to duck behind the roadside hedge when headlights and revving engine warned him of first a car, then a cement lorry. The lorry was a clue to the factory. Ribble Cement. When he'd been driven along the old Chatburn to Clitheroe road on childhood holidays, the cement factory had seemed nothing much more than a builder's yard.

Grindleton was quiet. An empty street and lights in two bedroom windows. What was the time? He looked at his watch. 12.15 a.m. He had guessed it was much earlier. He padded past a short string of houses and a corner shop, crossed a road and climbed a gate on to the fell.

As he trudged up the steep slope, the wind started to gust into his face. It was strong and cold and coming from the north-west. Up ahead dark cloud seemed to be gathering over the ridge for which he was heading.

The going grew harder as the slope grew steeper and he moved from pasture to the peaty surface of the fell. He paused to gain breath and looked back to see how well he had done. An extraordinary sight had opened up behind him. Far below, the Ribble valley was mapped out by thousands of dots of light that ran along the main roads like strings of bulbs in Blackpool illuminations. And, immediately below him, at centre stage, was a floodlit launching pad disguised as the Ribble Cement factory, its tall central tower waiting for a rocket to be wheeled alongside. He had turned round on a deserted fell and found himself facing Disneyland.

A gust of wind pushed hard at his back and nearly toppled him over. He turned, bent his head into the wind and forced himself uphill. He was now out on open fell and his ears were filled not with the reassuring chuckle of the river but the unremitting, irksome roar of the wind.

When he next glanced up, he saw what looked like a cloud of mist rolling over the ridge towards him. He took out his Silva compass and used it to take a bearing on the corner of the wood towards which he was heading. He got his reading just in time because the mist soon obliterated his mark and rolled down the fell towards him. Only it wasn't mist. It was gusting, penetrating rain. Rucksack off. Waterproof trousers out and on. Hood of anorak up. Rucksack back on. Then slow scrambling progress up the slope. Visibility was now so bad that he had no choice but to walk the bearing, picking a mark sometimes only twenty yards ahead—a rock, the edge of a gully, even a prominent tuft of grass—then walking to it.

Twice he stepped into marshy pools thinking they were firm grass and fell face down into the mud. The second time he clambered out he found a sheep staring at him as if relieved to find a creature more stupid than itself. The rain was unrelenting and, after every gust, seemed to increase its intensity.

Bill's morale sank low. He was getting nowhere, scrambling up barren fell twenty yards at a time with no confidence that he was anywhere near his original bearing. Then the ground started to slope not ahead but to his right. He had veered way off course. After those falls he must have made some stupid mistake reorientating himself. Now he had no confidence that he knew where he was. He stood in teeming rain in an unknown patch of open countryside, alone, weary, and depressed.

Then through the insistent noise of wind and rain he heard another sound, so faint he wondered if he imagined it. He moved across the slope and found a small brook cascading down the fellside with the same torrential fervour with which the rain was beating on his hood. And further down the slope the hand of man had placed a plank across the stream. He scrambled down to it and found traces of a path.

Holding his torch close to his map case, he tried to read the detail through a film of rain that ran across the plastic. He found the brook. He found the path. And, because miracles sometimes happen, he also found he was near the place he had chosen to camp when the map was spread on Big John's table.

The path led him zigzag up steep fell to the edge of the forestry plantation near the summit. He climbed the wire fence boundary and used his torch to pick his way some forty yards into the wood. The spruce gave better protection from the rain than he thought it would and he found a flat clearing in which to set up his tiny one-piece tent.

When the tent was pitched, he dug a thermos from his rucksack and, leaning against a tree and sheltered by thick branches overhead, poured out the soup he had heated on Big John's gas stove. Another dose of the ubiquitous Heinz tomato yet he relished each steaming mouthful as he listened to the wind and rain driving into the trees high above him. With his belly warm, he engaged in complicated manoeuvres to shed boots, waterproof trousers, and anorak, as he eased himself feet first through the narrow opening of his tent and into his dry sleeping-bag. He laid rucksack, boots, trousers and anorak, wet side out, neatly along one side of the tent, sleeping bag along the other.

He tied down the tent flap behind him, and pillowed his head on a sweater packed with socks and underclothes. The wind and the rain were now noises outside the tent. Inside the sleeping-bag he was warm, dry, and secure. Within seconds he was asleep.

The wipers swept at their maximum speed yet managed to achieve only fleeting patches of clarity in the rain that streamed down the windscreen.

"Hang on," said the man in the passenger seat.

"What's it now?" asked the driver.

"Back there on the verge. A white bundle."

"Probably the leftovers of somebody's picnic."

"I'd still like to take another look."

"Would you now?" said the driver.

He braked and changed into a lower gear. "No skin off my nose. You're the one who'll have to brave the monsoon."

The police car slowed to a stop and the driver turned to look out the rear window.

"Can't see a thing. Like travelling under water. Let's hope no one's coming up behind us with his lights off."

He reversed the car slowly.

"Hold on. There it is."

The driver stopped and, before he could speak, his passenger was out of the door and running along the grass verge. Within seconds he was back, carrying a bundle of papers neatly tied with string. He'd left the door open and he scrambled in and slammed it quickly after him.

The driver glanced at the bundle.

"Is that all it was? Hardly worth getting your uniform wet."

His companion was trying to decipher the rain-soaked print on the top sheet of the bundle.

"'Stannington Women Against Pit Closures'," he read. "'Protest meeting. Next Thursday in Doncaster.' Bit of a long-distance invitation for here."

"Litter louts," said the driver. "Sure it wasn't last Thursday?"

"No. Next Thursday. And there's a good hundred leaflets here."

"Never can tell with these loony women. Chuck 'em in the back and we'll dump 'em in the bin when we're on our break."

He flicked on his indicator, looked in the rear mirror, and pulled away from the kerb.

His companion riffled through the bundle.

"I wonder," he said. "They told us they wanted to hear of anything unusual. Nothing too trivial, they said."

Another riffle through the leaflets.

"Let's take them at their word."

He leaned over and picked up the radio handset.

Chapter Ten

The sergeant never quite knew where he was with the colonel. Those drooping eyelids made the old boy look as if he were about to drop off to sleep, and that soft voice meant you never could tell whether he was angry—which the sergeant thought he might be now—or happy, which he doubted the old bugger had ever been. So the sergeant did what he always did and stood smartly to attention in front of the colonel's desk.

"So what you are telling me, sar'nt, is that the only return we have from this elaborate and expensive exercise is one pair of wellington boots."

"Not quite, sir."

The sergeant gazed fixedly at a map on the wall some two feet above the colonel's head. Gazed at it but didn't see it. A focus point while he reeled off his prepared statement.

"We know he went into Stannington. We also know that the Embley woman went off on that long excursion on the afternoon he arrived. And we know where she went. She was in her own car. Morris Minor. Dark green. It was under observation all the way, and while it was parked. So if he was in the car, sir, which I doubt, we know he didn't get out.

"Then last night, Special Branch tipped us the wink that the Women's Loony van had been spotted on the A59 travelling east through Whalley. It's on their regular 'Report if seen' list. We got the boys in blue to flag it down before it could reach the M6. Empty. But when they checked the driver's ID who should it turn out to be but Madame Embley who our lads had logged as tucked up in her bed in Wilberforce Street.

"As soon as we heard that we went in. Her house and the old man's. Both as clean as a whistle. The old man wasn't best pleased. Caught one of our lads a nasty one over the eye with his stick. Said he thought he was a burglar."

"So we made a balls of it, sar'nt. For God's sake man, relax. You're not on the parade ground. Come and look at this."

The colonel swivelled in his chair towards the Ordnance Survey map pinned to the wall behind him. The sergeant moved awkwardly around the desk and the colonel picked up a Magic Marker.

"Now, sar'nt, there's Whalley."

He drew a small red circle on the map.

"And there's Stannington."

He drew another small circle.

"Join them together . . ."

He did.

". . . and let's see if we can find some thing or some person close to that line who might hold an interest for our man."

The sergeant showed willing by leaning forward and taking an exaggerated interest in the map.

"But first, sar'nt, I suggest you check whether anyone else has logged a routine sighting of that van. The more accurately we can plot its route the smaller will be our final circle on the map. Meanwhile, knowing what I do from his dossier, and until we get harder information, I suggest we move most of our men in here."

He drew a large red circle that encompassed Clitheroe, Slaidburn and the Forest of Bowland.

One o'clock. Bill packed up his gear and carried it to the edge of the wood that overlooked the Hodder valley. For a moment, until he grew used to the false perspective imposed by the height, the valley looked as unreal as a toyshop display of a model farm. The meadows by the river were too green, the sheep too carefully placed on the slopes of the fells, and the eight stone houses dotted erratically upon the lower slopes were surely made of plastic, just as surely as the black and white cows that stood in the fields were made of lead.

Then, as he watched, someone breathed life into the model. A cow moved, a sheep bleated, and smoke rose from the chimneys down at Broadhead and at Skelshaw.

He found a dry hollow, took off his rucksack and, using it as pillow, stretched out on his back on the turf. The sun was warm and he closed his eyes. The image of the valley persisted. Warmth, sunshine, trees on a river bank beginning to shed their leaves. A romantic evocation of Britain at war. Vapour trails across a summer sky. But whose Britain was he fighting for now? The thing that angered him most was being linked with biological warfare. That was wicked. Poor Alick Isaacs would be revolving in his grave.

Soon after he'd qualified, Bill had met Alick, and his Swiss friend Jean Lindemann, at their laboratory in Mill Hill where they'd just discovered Interferon, the substance human cells produce when they are invaded by a virus and which protects them from invasion by other viruses. There'd been great excitement then because in 1957 a lot of people thought every cancer was triggered by a virus and, if Interferon protected the cells against the virus, it could protect them against the cancer.

The excitement soon waned and, when Alick Isaacs died in 1967, people's interest in Interferon seemed to die with him. A few remained intrigued by the notion that the body might be stimulated to produce its own natural defence against cancerous growth; they isolated different forms of Interferon and, later, other natural chemicals which the body produces to defend itself. Their problem was that only human cells could produce the chemicals and, though scientists could isolate them in small quantities in laboratories, no one could produce enough to test them as anti-cancer agents.

Then along came bioengineering and the possibility of creating special cells to manufacture natural chemicals.

From across the fell he heard a car grinding in low gear down the narrow road from Waddington. It rattled across a cattle grid and moved, as a tiny black dot, across his horizon.

In Britain, some of the most productive bioengineering went on behind closed doors in defence laboratories, largely because it was the best funded. The first official secret to come Bill's way was entrusted to him back in the fifties when, during his national service, he'd been given an army pamphlet on nerve gases, the invisible poisons which paralyse the nervous system and cause the immediate death of anyone exposed to them. In 1986, the gases were still around, if only because attempts to produce antidotes had always been outpaced by refinements to the gases.

In the Seventies, the Ministry of Defence invested heavily in research to see if human cells might produce their own antidotes to nerve gases, in much the same way as they produce Interferon to protect themselves against viruses. The investment paid off when MOD scientists isolated just such an antidote. They named it Neurinterfer and sought ways to produce large enough quantities to test it as a protective. They got the bioengineers to insert specific human genes into the nuclei of *E coli* and discovered that, under the right conditions, these engineered bacteria produced Neurinterfer.

The conditions proved highly critical and, in one experiment, the bacteria produced a different substance which the scientists couldn't identify. They separated the aberrant strain of *E coli*, kept cultivating it, and eventually isolated the new substance, Neurinterfer 593. Though it gave no protection against nerve gas, it did protect against viruses.

Within months the scientists discovered that Neurinterfer 593 was not a single substance but a family of related chemicals, some of which seemed to have a powerful Interferon effect. Later, when reports started to appear in medical journals suggesting Interferon was a useful treatment for some cancers of the kidney, of the skin, of lymph glands, and of bone marrow, the MOD decided that the Neurinterfer 593s should be investigated.

The problem was that they had no obvious military value and defence research establishments are not geared to large clinical trials. Yet the MOD was reluctant to abandon the investment already made in the research, so it decided to go outside its usual scientific establishments and set up a new clinical research centre to exploit any biological products produced incidentally by defence research. The new centre's foundation project was the clinical investigation of the Neurinterfer 593s.

Sir Rex was a member of most of the Ministry's advisory committees so the Secretary of State appointed him director of the new centre and gave him the authority to recruit the team he needed. The MOD, which likes to keep its facilities in out-of-the-way places amenable to effective security, bought the old manor house at Gartridge in Cheshire, gutted and restructured its interior, and built new laboratories in the park.

It also expended a lot of committee time on giving the place a name. The committee gurus thought it would diminish the centre's "image" if it had too blatant a connection with defence so they settled eventually for the Government Liaison Scientific and Clinical Research Establishment. Everyone who worked there called it the Centre.

And that was how Bill and, for that matter, Kate and Paddy and Tim and Greg—all of them doing an honourable job in cancer research—were now being linked with biological warfare and "cloak-and-dagger research".

The air had grown still and the rustle of the branches in the wood behind Bill had faded away. Now another sound floated up from the fell below. Not sheep, nor car, nor cattle grid this time. The sound of laughter.

Two voices. A woman's laugh. And then a man's response. Too far away to catch the detail of what was said.

Bill rolled on to his stomach and crawled to the edge of his hollow. A man and a woman were walking across the fell, maybe half a mile away but following a track that would bring them within twenty yards of where he lay.

He lowered his head and slid down into his hollow. He lay on his back, raised one hand to his brow to shade his eyes from the sun, and listened as the voices came nearer. They came close enough for him to hear odd words but not words he could string coherently together. When the voices started to recede, he crawled back to the edge of the hollow and watched the backs of the walkers until they disappeared down the slope up which he'd climbed the night before.

He raised the glasses that hung from a strap around his neck and scanned Hodder Bank Fell. Sheep, a few cattle, but no more walkers.

He lazed for another ten minutes then stirred himself to set up his calor stove for what he hoped was the last time.

He waited superstitiously until the rim of the sun had disappeared into the Trough of Bowland before setting out on the last leg of his walk and, as he left the shelter of the wood and descended into the valley, he put up a snipe that rose almost from under his boot.

He paused to listen and heard only the rattling chatter of a pack of magpies who'd found something to fight over at dusk. He stepped briskly down the track, eager for the rhythm of the walk to take over.

That newspaper report still rankled. "Top secret defence project." Who allowed them to use words like that to describe clinical trials in which the only enemy was cancer? The trials were no different from all the others he'd been involved with at St Christopher's. He'd gone to the Centre on no secret mission but to do routine trials on one of the Neurinterfers: Neurgamma. They'd chosen that one because it had been the most promising in animal studies and in the studies Kate had done on volunteers.

True, the trials had come up with a surprise. Not a secret. Just a surprise. He was aware of the regular thump of his boots on the turf as his memory struggled to grasp something that was almost within its reach.

The early trials had gone well, and then they'd gone better, and then . . . Tom Winters had rung him. Tom worked in a hospital in Kent and was using the drug in patients who were also having radiotherapy. The trial was double-blind: half the patients were having injections of Neurgamma, the other half injections of a placebo, a fluid which looked like Neurgamma but contained no active substance. Neither the patients nor their doctors knew which injections they were having. They came in identical bottles marked only with a code number and the key to the code was in a sealed envelope in Bill's office. He would open the envelope only when the trial was over.

Tom had worked with Bill before and he rang that morning to say he could guess which of his patients were receiving Neurgamma because they suffered none of the side-effects from radiotherapy—the excessive tiredness or the nausea—suffered by those on the placebo.

Next morning Bill got the same message from a hospital in Cumbria. He went to see Tom and the other investigator and then he got back to the Centre contacted every hospital in the trial. He asked all investigators to record the names of patients who seemed to have been protected against radiotherapy side-effects and, only after the names had been lodged with him, did he open the envelope and break the trial code. The results were staggering. Nearly every patient who had no side-effects had been on Neurgamma.

He reached the foot of the valley. A near full moon had risen and he had little trouble finding the path that ran alongside the river. The going was easy and, since the snipe, the only creatures he'd encountered were suspicious yet incurious sheep.

When he'd told Rex about the findings they'd had a meeting of the whole research staff and devised a series of experiments to try to determine why Neurgamma seemed to protect patients against radiotherapy side-effects. It was an exciting time for all of them. They were no longer following up research done by others but were now involved in creative research of their own. Paddy Shaughnessy moved a camp-bed into his laboratory and rarely emerged save to splutter excitedly about how well everything was going.

Then, one evening at a rapidly convened meeting in the boardroom, a beaming Shaughnessy announced he had evidence, as near as dammit irrefutable, that Neurgamma, in some way he had yet to determine, protected normal cells against radiation. His even better news was that Neurgamma was not taken up by abnormal cells.

They bombarded one another with cautionary clichés about these being early days yet and how a lot could still go wrong but they found it hard to contain their excitement. If Shaughnessy's findings in animals were confirmed in human beings the implications for cancer treatment were enormous.

X-rays don't kill just cancer cells. They also kill healthy cells and can be used in treatment only because cancer cells are more susceptible to their damaging effect than normal cells. Their use is limited by the need to keep the dose low enough not to destroy too many healthy cells. If Neurgamma did what Shaughnessy said it did, patients protected by it could receive massive doses of radiation, enough to kill off all the cancer cells without doing any damage to healthy tissue.

Kate's Phase One tests in humans confirmed the effect and Bill set up a small-scale clinical trial. The results were exciting

104

Patients protected with Neurgamma *could* be given higher doses of radiation without apparent harm.

Those were days of high euphoria for the team; sure they were on to a great discovery but fearing all the time that something would go wrong. And then—he heard the echo of a phrase he had spoken to Big John—something did go terribly, catastrophically wrong.

He realized the rhythm of the walk had quietly restored another corner of his memory. Yet as soon as he grew conscious of it, the process stopped. He looked around him and discovered he had been walking under automatic pilot. He had kept away from the road, skirted the village at Dunsop Bridge, and was now on the last lap, the metalled track that ran alongside the Dunsop river.

The moon picked out the valley ahead of him in luminous detail save where trees or outcrops of rock cast solid black shadows. He was walking into a gorge and the steep fells that rose from each side of the river were clothed with dark trees.

8.45 said his watch. Two miles to go. If he could keep up this pace he should reach Marion's at 9.30 p.m. Ahead he thought he could see the crest of Middle Knoll, the fell that divided the gorge up which he was walking. Within a minute, his diagnosis was confirmed. The loom of headlights swung out of the black shadow beneath the crest. Then came the headlights themselves. Their light shone first down the valley, then swung to his left and charted the course of the track that ran across the lower slopes. The lights were a mile away and he had plenty of time to take cover. He moved on to rough ground to his left, found a hollow that was not too damp, and lay on his belly watching the approaching headlights. When they drew near, he lowered his face to the grass. The vehicle passed and, as he raised his head to look after it, he saw the shape of a Land Rover clearly outlined against the glare of its own headlights.

He got up and soon resettled in to the rhythm of his walk. After twenty minutes he reached the head of the valley and the sluices that control the merging of the Dunsop's two main tributaries. He crossed a bridge and after a hundred yards, when the track divided, took the left branch leading into a dale.

Up ahead he caught the first glimpse of journey's end, a twinkle of light that, as he drew nearer, he could see came from a window. The moonlight picked out the little cluster of buildings grouped at the foot of the fell: a long low farmhouse, a barn, a cottage, and a jumble of sheds. The track led him past a sheep pen and a walled garden and into the central yard. Beyond the buildings was barren fell rising to a steep crest. The only access to this place was along the route he'd walked. And now the walk was over.

Light came from every window in the lower storey of the farmhouse and, as he entered the yard, he heard music. An old gramophone record. Ray Noble and his orchestra and the voice of Al Bowlly.

> I long to be
> Beneath that Riviera Moon

He hammered on the door with the crook of his stick.

> Just wanna see
> That silvery balloon

As Al and Ray reprised the chorus, Bill thought he heard some movement on the other side of the door. A bolt was pulled, the door opened slowly, and Al Bowlly's crooning spilled through the gap and out on to the empty dale.

In the doorway stood a slim woman wearing a long black dress, ankle length, tight around the hips, fluffy at the neck. Her right hand held a stubby cigarette-holder between its fingers, her left clutched a glass. Her platinum hair was permed tight to her skull, and her thin eyebrows had been pencilled in an arch that was as exaggerated as the Cupid's bow shaped round her mouth in thick red lipstick.

She stared up into Bill's face, then shuddered, put her right hand to her mouth and clenched the knuckle of her forefinger between her teeth. She lowered her hand an inch and whispered: "Oh, my God, it's David."

"Sorry." Bill echoed her whisper. "Just his son."

Chapter Eleven

Bill sat in a deep armchair. At the far end of the room, his rucksack lay where he had dumped it, near the open door to the hall. As soon as he'd got it off his shoulders, he'd been sent across to the cottage to fetch an apple-cheeked woman called Myrtle who'd smiled her way across the yard and then gone upstairs with an armful of sheets and pillowcases.

Al Bowlly, rotating at seventy-eight revolutions per minute behind the glossy veneer of an old radiogram, was re-serenading the moon. From the kitchen, just an open door away, Marion crooned along with Al and her voice, counterpointed by crackling and sizzling, floated into the room on an aroma of fried food.

The voice was young. Yet she must be in her late sixties. Sheathe your calculator, Marsden. She greeted you warmly, she makes you feel safe, and her voice is young.

> Just wanna see
> That silvery balloon

Bill's leather chair had a twin at the other side of the brick fireplace: golden velvet cushions, an embroidered antimacassar, and, across one arm, a narrow leather strap with weighted stirrups at each end and a small brass ashtray at its centre.

> We said "Goodbye"
> For such sensible reasons.
> We feared the storms
> We knew
> Would stir
> The seasons . . .

Al and Marion crooned the melody into another key.

The room was long, and low, and crowded. Prominent figures

in the crowd included a chintz sofa, an oak dining-table, and a black boudoir grand, with sheets of music scattered across its lid. Beyond the piano, a glass-fronted cabinet was crammed with porcelain figures and two large dishes whose willow pattern echoed repeatedly from a plate rail tucked up beneath the bulging plaster and rough beams of the ceiling.

Below the rail, the walls were decorated only with photographs, hung so close together they obscured the texture behind them. No two were the same size but all were framed in identical black frames. Some were single portraits, more were groups. Most of the men had shiny black hair plastered down and parted; most of the women had their hair short and permed. Many of the subjects were in evening dress, a few of the men were in uniform. Bill's father, who stared at him from every corner, appeared most often in a tweed jacket.

The one wall free from photographs was the wall behind Bill. That was decorated with books. The lines of paperbacks started on the floor and reached to the ceiling save where the shelves that carried them had been cut and reinforced to form an arch around the kitchen door. Nearly all the books were Penguins, two thirds with orange covers, one third with green; a handful were blue Pelicans and there were a few gaudy intruders.

The last notes of Al's cadenza faded, another record slapped down from the stack Marion had placed on the chromium-plated spindle, and the Glenn Miller Orchestra and the Modernaires swung into the room.

Myrtle appeared in the doorway from the hall.

"I'm done now," she said, "So I'll say good-night."

And she was gone. Bill heard her close the front door behind her. Did the accent of these parts, more Lancashire than Yorkshire, really contain a lilt that signalled gentleness or had Bill been conditioned to associate it with gentle people?

Marion came through the kitchen door carrying a tray. Bill got up to help her.

"You stay where you are, young man. It'll be much easier if you don't fuss."

Her bossiness was unaffected. The men in her life had always known their place, which wasn't in the kitchen.

She put the tray on the dining-table.

"If you must do something, why not be a good boy and open this."

She handed him a champagne bottle and a napkin. He unwound the wire and started to lever the cork with his thumbs. Marion laid two places at the table. At one she placed a small plate carrying discreet portions of smoked salmon and scrambled egg; at the other, a large plate laden with eggs and bacon, fried bread, black pudding, and a Barnsley chop.

She handed Bill a glass.

"Better have this. I doubt that bottle's cool enough and it could have a premature ejaculation."

Her accent still had the light Yorkshire intonation that his father used to call high-quality Harrogate.

She lit a single candle at the centre of the table and went to turn off the room's only lights, a tall brass standard lamp in the corner and a reading lamp on a walnut table by the fire.

As the lights went out, the cork came free, and Bill caught the first flow in the glass.

"Clever boy," said Marion. "Now pour it out, sit yourself down, and get some solid food inside you."

In the background, Geraldo had taken over the bandstand. "Penny Serenade." Marion seemed oblivious to the music and, as they ate the first mouthfuls, she kept her eyes on Bill's.

"Delicious," said Bill, and he meant it.

Marion smiled.

"I recognize real hunger when I see it. Every so often when I've had a good day's walking on the fell, I treat myself to a fry-up like that. I'll switch off the music and let you concentrate."

She swung round in her chair and flicked a switch on the radiogram.

When she swung back, she raised her glass. Bill raised his and she clinked hers against it.

"Welcome," she said and emptied her glass in one swallow. Bill sipped from his and refilled Marion's.

There was silence while Bill ate and Marion nibbled. Then she laid down her knife and fork.

"I'd best say it now," she said. "There are certain rules attached to this house. You will notice I have no television set and the radio side of that machine has been disconnected. I also have no telephone and I take no newspapers. People who come here are expected to leave their news behind.

"I welcome a few friends, and you, young man, are the most welcome visitor I have had in years. But even with you, I don't want to hear where you've come from or why you're here."

"Big John Embley told me about the rules," said Bill.

"He's a good man, John. And he was a good friend of your father's. He and his daughter call on me nearly every year, usually on their way to Blackpool."

She carefully fitted the gold tip of a black Russian cigarette into a stubby meerschaum holder and lit it. Then she moved her chair back from the table and watched Bill eating, as if to ensure he was extracting every ounce of value from the food.

The cigarette had lost half its length before she spoke.

"You have the look of your father," she said.

She leaned across and topped up his glass before refilling her own.

"And you are allowed to *hint* at a little bit of news. I had heard you'd married a lovely young lady."

"Susie died five years ago," said Bill.

Marion spat a mouthful of smoke at the ceiling.

"Shit," she said, "if you'll pardon my French."

She seemed to bite hard on the holder as she took a deep inhalation.

"That's exactly why I won't let the world into this house. Outside there's nothing but bad news."

Another deep drag on her cigarette. Then she looked at Bill.

"Forgive me," she said. "How awful it must have been for you."

She placed her hand gently over his, and then withdrew it as if guilty of a social misdemeanour.

"But let's not talk about it . . ."

She looked at him anxiously.

". . . unless, of course, you want to."

Bill shook his head. Marion smiled and sipped from her

e world I knew with your father has gone and I don't like

what's replaced it. Much better to enjoy the past; especially as we were too rushed to enjoy it at the time."

She filled her glass once more and took it over to the piano.

"If you live as I do, you can filter out the nasty bits."

She sat on the long black stool and let her hands move gently along the keyboard, caressing the notes. At first they produced only soft chords but after a moment these resolved into a slow, sad melody—a melody Bill's father had once played over and over on the gramophone.

The song was called "You'll never know" and now Marion added the words in that small true voice.

Alice Faye was the first singer Bill had known by name. He poured himself another glass of wine and kept on eating.

December 1949. Bill was just seventeen and faced the first great drama of his life. He found a letter in his father's desk and ferreted the detail from a reluctant Jimmy Embley. His father had a fancy woman with platinum hair who lived on the posh side of Doncaster—a mysterious sophisticate who ran a dress shop in the High Street called "Estelle's".

One evening, after dinner, Bill the romantic hero, avenger of his wronged mother, staged a showdown in the sitting-room. His father sat subdued, eyes cast down, while Bill indulged in rhetorical denunciation that grew more flamboyant as it fed upon itself. Then Bill's mother cried, and Bill cried with her, and his father just sat there and said nothing.

Later his mother came and sat on the side of his bed, as she had done when he was a child, and explained that he was not to worry, that she knew all about his father. One day he would understand what she understood then. Meanwhile Bill should always remember how lucky he was to have such a kind and generous father who loved him so much.

Then she kissed Bill on the cheek and left the room.

His father had never spoken of that evening. After it they managed to contrive a *modus vivendi* based on suspicion and, though the tension between them eased, they kept one another at emotional arm's length for another two years—until Bill's mother died. She had been ill for just six months and her decline over the last four weeks had been precipitate.

On the night she died Bill's father wept in his son's arms and the emotional bond that had once held them so close together was reforged.

When Bill was midway through his second year at Cambridge, his father wrote to tell him that Marion had moved into the house but that they'd decided not to marry. Bill saw her during university vacations but he was too busy discovering people of his own age, and loving some of them, to have time to get to know her. She was a pleasant person who was about the place when he came home and, as he moved on through medical school, he returned to his father's house less often, and less often thought of it as home.

Marion repeated the chorus for the third or fourth, or was it the fifth time?

Bill had finished eating. As he stood, intending to take his plate to the kitchen, Marion played a loud dissonant chord.

"It's no bloody good, is it?" she said. "It's all gone and the memory is elusive."

She raised her hands from the keyboard, took another black cigarette from the silver box on the piano and fitted it into the meerschaum holder. She lit it with the onyx lighter that stood on the piano, then turned and smiled at Bill.

"Don't worry. I indulge in an occasional outburst. Fill your glass and then fill mine. And leave all that stuff on the table. Myrtle will clear it in the morning."

She got up from the piano and sat in the armchair opposite Bill's. The only light came from the candle on the table and a smouldering log on the hearth. Bill filled her glass and sat opposite her.

"Don't know how long you want to stay," she said, "but you can have a room here for as long as you need. There's a car in the barn, if you want to use it. George Liversedge—that's Myrtle's husband—takes me out in it sometimes. Not often because I have everything I want around me here, in this house and up there in the dale.

"The car's rather grand. The Tiddeley Armstrong your father always called it. There are curtains in the back and—I know this sounds batty but it's true—if we do go out, I keep them drawn until we get to where we're going. Ingleborough. The top of Longridge Fell. It's a sort of magic transporter that cuts out the nasty bits in between.

"Those are the only times I leave the dale. George and Myrtle do my shopping and they know what I want to hear and what I don't. My rules are not a game. When your father died, I saw the world going rotten and I refused to go rotten with it."

She picked up the champagne bottle and leaned forward to pour what was left into Bill's glass. Bill shook his head in refusal and she emptied the bottle into her own.

"Let me make two things clear," she said. "I'm not a crazy old lady and I'm not a drunk. Though there are evenings when I drink too much."

She raised her glass and offered Bill a smiling toast.

"And tonight I have a better excuse than I have had for years."

The sergeant put the bedraggled bundle of leaflets on the desk.

The colonel picked it up and looked at the top one.

"Standard feminist loony," he said.

"Stannington Women Against Pit Closures, sir. Same leaflets as they found in the van when they stopped it last night. These come from a grass verge on the A59 just outside Chatburn."

Even now he couldn't tell whether the old bugger was pleased. Those sleepy eyes produced no response.

"We've been to have a look. Tyre tracks on the grass. Two deep skid marks that look as though they were made by the heels of a pair of boots. We reckon he jumped out of the van and the leaflets came with him."

Still no response.

"Seems, sir, your hunch was right and we've got our men into the right area."

The colonel swivelled his chair and looked at the map.

"I drew that circle, sar'nt, because that's where his family comes from. His grandfather was a doctor in Slaidburn. Let's check to see if he has any relatives left up there."

The sergeant glanced at the clock on the wall.

"Now, sir?"

"Why not? Set the night shift to work on the directories and maps. And make sure they work hard."

"Very good, sir."

The colonel stared intently at the red circle on the map.

"He's in there somewhere, I'm damned sure. And, this time, there's no way that he's going to get out."

He turned suddenly and barked at the sergeant.

"Am I right, sar'nt?"

For a moment the sergeant was genuinely scared by the look in the old boy's eyes.

"Oh yes, sir. You're quite right, sir. This time he's not going to get away."

"We bought this place for his retirement," said Marion.

"He always said he'd come back," said Bill. "My grandfather died before I was born but, every year during the war, we took a cottage near Dunsop Bridge for our summer holidays."

Marion picked up the poker from the hearth and prodded at a smouldering log. A flurry of sparks flew up the chimney.

"David and I spent the whole of June here in that marvellous summer of 1976, the one that everyone remembers. He was due to retire at the end of the year and we were going to come back for Christmas and live out the rest of our lives together. Make up for all those days when we were young and had to play hide-and-seek with the rest of the world."

She looked at Bill as if waiting for a response. It didn't come.

"And then, the afternoon after we went back to Stannington, he got a pain in his chest. He wouldn't let me call anyone to see him but drove off to do his evening surgery. Do you know what the last words were that I spoke to him? I shouted after him as he went through the door: 'You're a stubborn old fool, my darling.'"

She drank what was left in her glass.

"Now I *am* a little drunk," she said.

She stared uncertainly at Bill.

"Would you do me one great favour?"

Bill hesitated and she took his silence for acquiescence. She got up and went over to the radiogram.

She knew exactly where to find the record she wanted. She cleared the others from the spindle, placed it on the turntable, and flicked the switch. This time it was Alice Faye herself who

114

sang. Marion crossed the room and extended her arms to Bill. For a moment Bill was puzzled. Then he understood.

He got out of the chair, and raised his arms.

Alice Faye. "You'll never know". The Gaumont cinema. His father's gramophone.

They danced slowly around the room, moving formally like a couple on an old time dance floor.

Then Marion rested her cheek on Bill's shoulder, her head nestling against his neck.

The candle on the table was now just a pool of melted wax and, as they brushed past, it flickered and went out.

Beyond the windows lay the moonlit fells, and beyond them the confusion that Bill could not understand. Why bother to try? Here was comfort and warmth and a fellow human being seeking refuge. He held Marion and kept on dancing.

Chapter Twelve

Bill awoke in an Enid Blyton illustration. The walls of his bedroom were sunshine yellow, the wooden furniture was pastel blue, and his bed was covered with a patchwork quilt. Beyond the red check curtains, which he had left undrawn, and the leaded windows, which he had left open, the sky was a cloudless blue and the rolling slopes below Brennand Fell echoed the quilt with patches of green, and brown, and misty blue. Somewhere beyond the window and out of his sight two crows were having an argumentative caw. Much closer was the sound of water hurrying across stones. Somewhere between came the insistent bleating of sheep.

The sun had long been up. The red clock on his bedside table told him it was 9.30. He swung his legs out of bed, padded to the door, and opened it. The house was silent. At the far end of a landing rendered low and narrow by the slope of roof beams, Marion's door was closed but the door of the bathroom he had used the night before was open.

Twenty minutes later, bathed and shaved, with clean underwear against his skin and soft sneakers on his feet, he made his way downstairs. The only sounds he heard were the sounds of the house itself—ticking clocks, a gurgle in a pipe, the creak of a door on its hinges—amplified by the silence that surrounded them. Yet some busy person had cleared away the disorder they had left the night before. The room was tidy but not aggressively so; there was still a scatter of sheet music along the piano and a disorganized pile of green paperbacks on the floor beside one chair: Dorothy Sayers, John Dickson Carr, Margery Allingham. The windows were open and a drifting breeze from the fell had swept away all trace of last night's cigarette smoke.

The kitchen too was tidy. And a surprise. More like a farmhouse kitchen in a Sunday supplement than in a farm house: fitted cupboards, built-in electric hobs and oven, "working surfaces", a double-barrelled stainless-steel sink, frying pans hung on the wall to show off their copper bottoms, and a profligacy of sealed teak. Transparent resin covered the stone flags and filled the gaps between them to produce a smooth moppable surface. A stone floor in aspic. The room confirmed Bill's impression that Marion's notion of hermitage was more hedonist than penitential.

He made some tea and toast, poured himself a bowl of cereal, and, when he'd eaten, washed bowl, cup, saucer, and cutlery at the sink, drying them with a tea-towel inscribed with a recipe for Colonial Curry Tiffin.

The kitchen door was on the latch and, when he opened it, he discovered the source of the sound of which he'd been aware during the night whenever he stirred from his dreamless sleep. The end of the yard he had crossed in the moonlight had been flat but on this side of the house it tipped steeply as it elided with the slope of the fell. Its boundary was formed not by a stone wall but by a channel of large rocks, green with moss, through which a stream had been diverted to form tumbling waterfalls.

He walked round the corner of the house, stepping from shadow into warm sun. On the far side of the yard, the cottage from which he had fetched Myrtle was still and silent but a thin plume of smoke rose from one of its two chimneys. Beyond the cottage the sheep pens were now packed with a bleating crowd and, outside the pens, three dogs lay on bellies, silent but alert. In among the sheep a short broad-shouldered man pushed through the crowd, occasionally grabbing a sheep by its horns and forcing it through a narrow spring-loaded gate that separated one pen from the other. When he saw Bill, he pushed his way towards the side of the pen, taking a pipe from his pocket with an eagerness that suggested he was pleased to have an excuse to relight it.

The relighting took but one match and three brisk puffs.

"Nice morning," he said before puffs four and five.

Bill nodded assent.

"Don't know what they've done with this bloody weather," said the man.

Must be Myrtles's husband. George was it?

"We could have done with a bit of this . . ."

Another puff.

". . . in August."

"Looks like hard work lugging those sheep around."

"Hard work's already been done by those lads."

He waved his pipe at one of the dogs and got a vigorous burst of tail wagging in return.

"Getting 'em penned is what takes the time."

"Are you picking out some for the market?"

"Nothing like that. Separating the lambs from the ewes. Been on 'em now for four months and the old ladies are due for a rest. Once they're separate we'll have 'em back on the fell. One lot right over there and one in the field back here."

Three more puffs while he looked around his charges.

"Did Mrs Marsden tell you there were a car in the barn?"

Odd that she used her "courtesy title". She'd never used it when his father was alive.

"Too nice a day to be stuck in a car," said Bill. "I fancy taking a walk up there."

He pointed towards Whins Brow.

"If I were you," said George, "I'd go up t'other side."

He waved his pipe at Middle Knoll.

"It'll not be so wet and sun'll follow you round."

"Thanks for the advice," said Bill, and went back to the house. His boots were in the hall. He put them on, took his stick from the hall-stand, and set off across the yard. George still stood at the side of the pen, pipe in mouth, while he wiped his steel-rimmed spectacles with a handkerchief. He replaced the spectacles as Bill came out and watched him with a studious intensity. Bill broke the spell by giving George a wave. George returned it and moved reluctantly back in among his flock.

Bill climbed across one of the rocky waterfalls at the side of the yard and followed the stream up the side of the fell. As he climbed, he rounded the northern slope of Middle Knoll into another valley where the path descended sharply toward Whitendale.

Below him a cluster of farm buildings stood alongside the river and two Land Rovers, one hauling a trailer, were pulling into the yard. Bill stepped off the path and lay on his belly in a hollow to see what happened next. He cursed himself for not bringing his glasses.

Two men got out of the first Land Rover, one from the second, and all three went into the house. After interminable minutes, four men emerged from the house. One climbed into the driver's seat of the Land Rover with the attached trailer and backed it into a corner of the yard. Then the other three lowered the back of the trailer to form a ramp down which came a crowd of sheep jostling each other into a pen. Not only George had decided the time had come to sort ewes from lambs.

Bill climbed from his hollow and continued down the path. Incipient paranoia was the diagnosis. The world was going about its business and not everyone was engaged in the hounding of William Marsden. He felt the same sweet–sour blend of relief and disappointment he had known on the first day of his final medical examinations when he'd walked through streets full of people engaged in their routine tasks while he was on his way to meet his destiny.

As he descended he saw that the path led to a narrow footbridge across the river and, just beyond the bridge, would take him within yards of the farm buildings. He rehearsed the greeting he would offer the men, the traditional "hello" of the enthusiastic walker, but by the time he reached the farm the sheep had been penned and the men had gone indoors. As he passed he saw that both Land Rovers had the same sign painted on their doors: "North West Water".

Beyond the farm the path divided, and he turned right and walked towards the sun along Whitendale. He crossed one narrow stream and came to a deep cleft in the fellside. The path rounded the edge of the cleft and brought him to Costy Clough, a torrent that cascaded down Dunsop Fell. Below him, its fall was broken by a flat ledge from which sprang green trees and bushes nourished by its passing. The path zigzagged down to the ledge and, at its centre, a slab of concrete bridged the tunnel worn by the water. Bill paused at the centre of the bridge and looked up at the sheet of water that fell from the rocks into the whirling pool below.

The sound and sight of the falls filled his mind leaving no room for thought. Were he a psychiatrist seeking to assuage anxiety he would build his clinic overlooking moving water.

Eventually he moved away, reluctantly, and sat on a rock at the side of the ledge. The sun was warm on his shoulders, the dale below was empty save for disinterested sheep, and for the first time since he awoke in that bizarre clinic his mind felt sharp enough to disentangle reality from illusion. Thanks to his friends—though, in truth, they were his father's friends—he had found refuge. Now he had to determine what he sought refuge from.

The walk through Dovedale seemed a good place to start because it was easy to understand. Or was it? He was running away and he had been caught. That was a simple, straightforward explanation. Yet doubt niggled at it. Not all the data in his brain had been corrupted by the fall and a lingering fragment suggested he hadn't been running away but running towards. He was on his way to a meeting, a meeting that in some way involved a fox. But details like where, why, with whom, and what the hell a fox had to do with it, seemed irretrievable.

The problem with the "clinic" was different. He could remember everything that happened but could make no sense of it. Clearly it was no clinic, just a house to which they'd taken him to keep him under observation till he recovered from his concussion. But why dress it up as a clinic? And that intravenous drip and the monitor had been real. He had walked into a plot by John Buchan or Edgar Wallace, quite acceptable as a delusion. But he couldn't dismiss it as a delusion because reality had gone in with him. That doctor had been real enough and so had Sir Rex. The world's greatest actor could not have mimicked the essential egregiousness of Sir Rex.

But what was Rex doing inside Bill's delusion? And why had Bill suddenly panicked when he'd heard a voice in the room across the hall? That was a piece of the jigsaw that refused to fall into place. Why should just the sound of a voice cause the release of a deluge of adrenalin and compel him to tramp across Derbyshire? He should save that question for the men in the white coats when they came to take him away.

Better to do what he did the last time he tried to retrieve lost data. Return to Life before the Fall. Life at the Centre. There was a room there that seemed important. A long low room on the second floor. Built in one of the old bedrooms but with the ceiling lowered, the cornices stripped away, the window obscured by a venetian blind. Strips of fluorescent light, cork tiles on the walls and pictures formed of squiggles in primary colours, a long central table, rosewood veneer, chairs in speckled brown moquette. The board room they called it though, as far as any of them knew, they had no board. Rex sat at the head of the table. To his right sat a secretary taking shorthand notes, then Wilkinson, then Kate; to Rex's left sat Shaughnessy, then Craddock, then Bill. Bill was directly opposite Kate but she was determined not to catch his eye.

Tim Craddock, bless him, was speaking.

"I find it intolerable that, in any circumstances, we should be prevented from writing letters to our own professional journals. But this isn't just a routine letter. The data we've got suggest we've developed a substance which won't just relieve symptoms but gives genuine hope of lengthening and improving the quality of thousands of lives. And you tell us we can't publish our results."

"My dear Tim. Of course I understand your strength of feeling."

Rex's tone was that of the reasonable man.

"I wouldn't be a doctor if I didn't. But I have to remind you that we did all sign the Official Secrets Act when we signed our contracts and we're all intelligent enough, I hope, to have understood the implications of what we were doing."

"Can I make a comment?"

The rasping Queensland tone of Wilkinson.

"As I understood it when we met last month, you said that there was no question of our suppressing these results for ever . . ."

Rex nodded.

". . . but that they had to be screened by Security before they could be published."

Rex nodded again.

"That seems fair enough to me," said Wilkinson.

Bill saw Shaughnessy nod in agreement and felt it was time to intervene.

"Last month the colonel couldn't tell us how long that screening would take. Now Security has been sitting on them for eight weeks. Have they given you any idea how long it will be before they give us clearance to publish?"

"My dear Bill, it's not a matter of what you call clearance."

Rex was a schoolmaster dealing patiently with an irksome pupil.

"It may be that the defence implications of this work are so great that it will have to be kept under wraps for quite some time."

Bill snapped back.

"Then perhaps you'd like to explain to our complacent colonial over there just how many years add up to 'quite some time'."

The rudeness, though prompted by anger, was a mistake. Wilkinson continued to doodle on his notepad and Rex was off the hook.

Shaughnessy made a smiling intervention.

"It does seem to me that we may be getting a premature twist in our knickers. I'm as concerned as Bill that these results be published as soon as possible . . ."

"Aren't we all?" interpolated Rex as though enunciating one of the Great Truths that mankind has forgotten.

Shaughnessy ignored the interruption.

". . . but I don't see the point in making a fuss now before we know exactly what we're fussing about. I think you, sir, should put the screws on Security to give us some sort of time-scale and, if we think they're being unreasonable, that will be the time to complain."

Why did Kate sit immobile, staring at the pad in front of her? He knew she agreed with him but she sat there and said nothing. Now the bloody woman was bringing her prick-teasing antics to work with her.

Tim Craddock leaped in again.

"Can I remind you all of the reason why I asked Sir Rex for this meeting? It was not to discuss, yet again, the suppression of our results but to seek an explanation of how a private letter written by a senior member of the medical staff came to be intercepted by Security."

"My dear Tim, that's a rather dramatic way of putting it. You could say that Security has done Bill a good turn. If the *Lancet* had published that letter, he could now be facing a serious charge under the Official Secrets Act."

"Well I think it's a poor bloody show that all our letters are obviously being opened and censored."

Tim too had brought too much anger with him. Rex smiled benignly.

"Don't you think that's a mite paranoid? After all that's been said over the past few weeks should it surprise us that Security grow uneasy when they find an envelope in the mail-room addressed to the editor of the *Lancet*?"

Bill was learning. He didn't speak now but he wondered if Rex knew that he hadn't posted the letter in the Centre's mailbox but in the postbox in the village. The next letter, which he'd already written, would be delivered by hand to the *Lancet* offices tomorrow afternoon when he went up to town.

Rex looked slowly round the table, as if assessing the mood of his audience but in truth gathering their attention.

"I'm afraid this incident has produced some unfortunate sequelae. Up to now Security has treated us as honourable professional men . . ." he glanced at Kate, ". . . eh persons. But unfortunately we have not justified the trust they placed in us."

He didn't look at Bill.

"As a result I fear that we are all, to use the army vernacular, confined to barracks. Security has declared a 48-hour alert and, during that time, no one will be allowed to leave the Centre without a pass signed by me and countersigned by the colonel. It's a drastic step, I'm afraid, and one I fought hard against, but in the end I had to admit that tighter security was the only way we could ensure that individuals honoured the commitment to secrecy they have already given in writing. The 48-hour clampdown may sound draconian but the colonel has persuaded me it is essential."

"Bloody hell," said Shaughnessy. "I'm buggered if I'm going back to boarding school. You can have my resignation now."

Sir Rex smiled sadly.

"I'm afraid you're too late. The order's already been signed. And even if you resign you will have to remain here until the forty-eight hours are up. Security need that time to introduce the measures they deem essential. All work at this centre is now the subject of a D-notice which means that newspapers and television will make no mention of it. They, unlike it seems some people working here, have been convinced that keeping our findings under wraps is vital to our national defence."

"What on earth have they been told?" asked Bill.

"That is the colonel's department. Though I should point out that one of the joint chairmen of the Defence, Press and Broadcasting Committee which issues D-notices is the Permanent Secretary of our own department, the MOD. The media, I am told, will respect the D-notice because they know that any breach of it would be construed as a breach of national security and I should add that, on this occasion, editors of medical publications have also been issued with the notice."

"There are newspapers and journals in other countries," said Bill.

"That is one of the reasons why Security need their forty-eight hours."

Rex looked down at a typed sheet on the table.

"Meanwhile, the colonel wishes me to brief you on two other matters. First, Members of Parliament. If any of you consider approaching an MP you should be aware that, because the project on which we are engaged has a budget of less than two hundred million pounds, it does not have to be disclosed to the Public Accounts Committee, and it has not been so disclosed. As far as Parliament is concerned, the Centre and our work does not officially exist. Any MP who makes inquiries will receive assurance from the topmost level that the secrecy of this project is essential for national security and if he . . ."

"Or she," whispered Kate. Her only intervention.

". . . tries to carry the matter further, he will be met with an official denial that we exist."

Another glance down at the sheet of paper.

"The second matter the colonel asked me to raise is a more delicate one. I happen to think that because we are all members

124

of an honourable profession, each of us will in future respect the solemn contractual undertaking we gave when we signed the Official Secrets Act. If, however, any of our number should feel tempted to breach that agreement by seeking to talk to journalists or to send information abroad, the colonel has asked me to make it clear that not only will that person be subjected to rigorous prosecution under the Act, but Security will not hesitate to release information from the traitor's personal dossier or indeed any other information that might discredit their reliability as a witness."

"*Heil* Hitler," said Greg.

He got up from the table and when he spoke his voice was as calm and unhurried as it always was.

"If it interests you at all, *Sir* Rex," he put a rasping emphasis on the title, "I don't give a stuff for your official permission. I intend to walk out of this room, out of this house, and down the drive, and if any khaki pom tries to stop me going through the gate, he'll have to answer for it in Canberra."

"Sit down."

The sharpness of the command barked by Rex was so unexpected that Greg paused in his stride.

Rex was pale and tight lipped.

"I thought I was dealing with mature people. But clearly I was wrong. Let me remind you gentlemen"—this time there was no polite deference to Kate—"that the defence of this country is not a game. It may look like a panel game each week on *Panorama* or *World in Action* but you and I live in a real world that's tough and nasty and in which we have to keep ahead of an enemy who, if they could tip the balance, would happily overwhelm us.

"The only reason we've had peace in Europe for the past forty years is because we've been fighting a secret war, a war in which nasty things are done in our name in private. It ill becomes those of us who have enjoyed the benefits that war has won to strike moral attitudes at its expense."

"I didn't sign on for a war," said Shaughnessy. "I signed on to do medical research."

"We're all signed on whether we like it or not," said Rex.

"Of course, we're excited because Neurgamma could—and we still haven't enough data to do more than speculate—make radiotherapy a more accurate and effective treatment."

"Or put another way," said Greg, "could save the lives of lots of people who are dying younger than they need."

Rex didn't bother even to look at him but continued in his crisp no-nonsense voice.

"But our masters see Neurgamma in a different light. If it does protect healthy cells against radiation, they could use it to inoculate troops against the fall-out from tactical weapons. We might even be able to protect the whole population against radiation after a major nuclear incident. Certainly we could protect key personnel. Even limited protection would tip the balance in our favour in the war of deterrence that our masters have to wage."

Now he looked at Greg.

"And in terms of saving lives, if they can keep the balance in our favour, they will save millions where we might expect to help thousands."

"All very interesting," said Greg, "but I seem to recall that Russians suffer from cancer too. So if we use it on our patients and they use it on theirs, your jolly old balance can stay where it was before we started. I vote we just get on with treating the sick and leave this balancing business to the rocket makers and Hopalong and his Star Wars."

He turned and went to the door. When he opened it he found his way blocked by a soldier holding a black machine gun diagonally across his body.

"Bloody hell," said Craddock. Shaughnessy half rose from his seat then settled back. Kate, inexplicably, kept staring at the pad in front of her.

Bill remembered the fences and the television cameras round the park outside and the tall thin woman in East Berlin.

Greg turned from the door and thoughtfully rubbed his chin. Then he looked at Bill.

"Come on, Bill," he said. "Tell me I'm hallucinating."

The frame froze. Greg stood there immobile, fixing Bill with a disconcerting stare, as if pleading for an answer. And, as in all still frames, the image was slightly out of focus.

Bill closed his eyes but the memory tape refused to move on.

He screwed his eyes tighter, clenched his jaw, and tried to force his brain to concentrate. But all he captured was another image snatched from the moment he fell into the void from the rocks above Dovedale. Tim Craddock, moist cheeked, embracing him and Bill turning on his heel and walking away.

After that the screen went blank. The sound-track now was the rush of the fall behind him, the song of a thrush which sat high in a tree beside Costy Clough, sheep bleating in the distance. And Bill was aware that he was being watched. Under scrutiny from not too great a distance.

He opened his eyes and found his instinct had played him true.

A young couple stood on the bridge below the fall. They had turned their backs on the cascading water and were staring at Bill. When he opened his eyes, they walked off the bridge towards him and, as they drew near, both said "hello".

They passed him and followed the path that led round the edge of the ravine and out of his sight. Were they the same couple who had gone by yesterday as he lay in his hollow?

They looked much like them but he wasn't certain. Watch the paranoia, doctor. It's a notoriously insidious disease. Even if they were the same couple, their reappearance could be an innocent event. This would be a natural place for them to visit if they were exploring the area.

He picked up his stick from where he'd rested it on a rock and walked back across the bridge, intending to return to Marion's farm along the path that had brought him here.

The buoyancy had gone from his step and walking had become a chore. The man who had walked this path an hour before had been eager to retrieve a memory; now it was half retrieved, he was unsure that he wanted to know more. Till now he had assumed that bits of his memory had been knocked from his brain by the fall down the cliff. Now he had an uneasy suspicion that the fall was an irrelevance, that all the memories were still there but repressed by fear.

The sun had moved to the south and the path from Whitendale was in the shadow of Middle Knoll. He re-emerged into sunlight only when he reached the cluster of springs which were the fount of the stream that ran eventually beneath his bedroom window.

When he felt the sun's warmth on his shoulders his spirits started to rise. The patchwork dale was laid out below him and he could pick out the farmhouse buildings: the cottage, the main house, the barn. No sign of human activity there.

But there was human activity on the slope below him. A solitary man, moving far too swiftly to be George, was climbing the path towards him. Bill scrambled back towards the only cover the fellside offered, a low ridge that ran across the slope.

Again he cursed himself for leaving his glasses in his room. All he could do was lie behind the ridge and feel foolish. His undignified scramble must have been visible to the man below. Bill lay on his belly and, raising his head till he could just see above the ridge, watched the shape take on an identity as it grew nearer. Green tweed jacket, fawn trousers tucked into green socks. No hat. Fair hair.

Bill stood. Not a man but Marion, climbing the slope with an easy stride that gave no sign of effort or of strain.

Bill scrambled down towards her. As soon as she saw him, she stopped and waited.

"George told me which way you'd gone," she said. She wasn't even out of breath.

"I'm on my way back," said Bill.

She turned and looked back down the dale.

"What do you think of my valley now you can see it as it should be seen?"

Bill followed her gaze.

"Don't want to debase it with words," he said.

Marion turned to him, smiling.

"You are a polite fellow," she said. "Came to fetch you because I want George to drive us over to Little Bowland. We can take a picnic."

Then she set off down the slope with Bill trailing behind her picking his steps carefully.

When the slope grew gentler, Marion waited for him and, as he caught up, she took his arm and they strolled slowly toward the farm. She explained the plans she'd been making, th places they would visit, the walks they would take, over the next few days.

The gate into the yard was made of aluminium tubing and, when Bill slammed the bolt behind them, he provoked an echoing clang. The sound brought Myrtle to the door of her cottage and she crossed the yard towards Marion.

"You've got a visitor, ma'am," she said. "Least it's really a visitor for . . . eh . . ." She nodded at Bill. "Mr Marsden. Said I didn't know as how long you'd be. Happy to wait. Waiting in t'house."

Bill looked desperately around the yard and down the track. No cars. No lorries. They would be parked down the dale. There was only one exit from this place and they would be sitting there. He heard the rattle of a latch behind him and he turned. The door of the house opened and standing in the shadow beyond it was his visitor.

"Good afternoon, doctor," said the visitor. "Long time no see."

Bill turned to Marion.

"Marion," he said, "let me introduce you to Kate."

Chapter Thirteen

The world paused for an instant while Bill drew breath.

"What brings you here?" he asked.

"The same things that brought you, I think . . . I hope."

Kate tilted her head slightly to one side. Then smiled.

"As every good defector says, I chose freedom."

Marion stepped briskly forward and started to organize. Kate
was embraced and led indoors. Myrtle was sent to fetch tea and
cakes, and Kate struggled to stem the rush of Bill's questions.

No, she was sure no one had followed her. Yes, she agreed
that she was not exactly an inconspicuous figure but she was
still certain she had not been followed. Yes, the colonel's men
had tried to keep tabs on her but they had failed. Maybe when
Bill heard how she had covered her tracks he would under
stand. If he must know, she had come by train to Preston, bu
to Clitheroe, taxi to Whitewell, and had stayed the night in a
pub. Then she had walked. But it wasn't quite as simple a
that. And please, please, please, if he would give her time sh
would explain exactly why she was sure she had led no one t
the farm. Just as she would tell him what had happened at th
Centre after he left.

"I understand not one word that either of you has spoken,
said Marion. "And I'm not so sure that I want to."

Her smile was directed at Kate.

"Bill knows my feelings about involvement with the worl
outside this place. I'll leave him to explain them."

She stood.

"Not that they're absolute. If you want to talk to me, the
do. But I'll not be offended if you don't."

Then she went upstairs and left Kate and Bill alone with th
Earl Grey, the bone china, and the Dundee cake.

"I like her," said Kate. "Not at all how I imagined her. D
you know how cruel you were when you talked about her? Y

I guessed you'd go to her. She was top of my list. If I hadn't found you here my next stop would have been Stannington."

"I didn't go to her. I was sent. How on earth did you find her?"

"Manchester public library. You told me she lived in this part of the world when you sent her Christmas cards. Remember?"

She produced the mocking smile she seemed to reserve especially for him.

"I reckoned if she were still alive, she wouldn't have moved. Thought I'd reckoned wrong when I tried the phone books. Lots of Marsdens in these parts but no Marion. Rang three of them but they'd never heard of her. So, as a last fling, I tried the postal directory and there she was. Marsden, Marion. Laithe End Farm. When I got to Whitewell the landlord showed me where it was on his map."

"And why have you come?"

Kate put down her cup, raised her eyes and stared coolly into Bill's. Then her head tilted, as it had before, and she smiled.

"The answer to that may come later," she said. "First I need to know about this other Mr Marsden I keep reading about in the papers. The missing Top Doc who could help the police with their inquiries."

"Don't know the fella," said Bill. "I was hoping you would tell me. There's a lot I'm hoping you'll tell me. I can't even remember leaving the Centre."

Kate frowned.

"I've been tramping across the bloody countryside, crippled by amnesia . . ." The timbre of his voice grew uncertain, distorted by odd harmonics. "I fell down a cliff and they said I had concussion but they buggered me about. I'm slowly working things out but they still don't make sense. It's damned hard work and, God knows, at times I may have been hallucinating. So please don't ask me to explain things to you. I want you to explain them to me."

Kate said nothing. She stood and took his hands in hers. Then she kissed the back of each of his hands, turned them over, and brushed each palm with her lips. Then she pulled his arms around her and laid his head in the hollow between her breasts. Bill's self-pity drained slowly away.

They went into the tiny garden and sat on the rocks beside the stream and, while the sunlight weakened as its source descended towards Winfold Fell, Bill told Kate everything he remembered up to that moment when Wilkinson's face froze in a still frame.

When Bill reached the end of his tale, the last of the sunlight still loomed behind Winfold. Kate sat silent for a moment. Then she stood, turned away from him, and gazed across the darkening dale.

"I think I can make a guess at what's been happening," she said.

She turned to him, smiling.

"The good news is that I know enough to persuade you you've not been hallucinating. The bad news is that I don't know enough to explain it all."

She shivered.

"Can we go inside? It's getting cold out here for a delicate soul who hasn't been roughing it on the fells."

She put her arm through his and started to lead him back to the house. Suddenly Bill realized she had taken the initiative in every exchange they had ever had. The thought provoked an instinctive revolt. He stopped and grabbed her clumsily like an impetuous adolescent.

His voice rasped aggressively: "I'm not a fucking invalid, you know. I don't need a nursemaid."

Then he squeezed his body tight against hers, forced his thigh between hers, explored her mouth with his tongue. She didn't struggle. Indeed she seemed to respond but, when Bill drew his face away, the dusk light revealed a mocking smile.

"Feeling better, Sir Jasper?" she asked.

She disentangled herself, kissed him gently on his forehead took his hand, and led him inside. And like a scolded child he followed.

They found Marion sitting by the fire reading. Myrtle was in the kitchen producing lots of steam that drifted though the doorway. Marion got up.

132

"Myrtle's done her stuff upstairs," she said. "Let me show you your room, my dear, and the 'arrangements'."

As they went through the door, Kate turned to Bill.

"After dinner," she said, "I'll fill the gaps in the story. But only after dinner."

And now dinner was over and with it the embargo Kate had imposed. She and Bill sat in the leather chairs beside the hearth. Marion sat at the piano, playing quietly. She didn't sing, just hummed a melody to herself. The table was cluttered with empty plates and glasses. The logs in the hearth flared and crackled and sent petals of ash up the chimney.

"A bit like the dénouement in an Agatha Christie," said Kate. "After dinner the characters assemble in the drawing-room and the butler is summoned to lock the door. Our problem is we have no butler and only one character. And he can't remember what he's done. So maybe that's where we should start."

She hadn't been looking at Bill but gazing at the spluttering logs. Now she raised her head and, as she had that afternoon, fixed him with a cool stare.

"Your problem, doctor, is a simple one. When you walked out of the Centre, you took with you six seed cultures of the doctored *E coli* which produce our precious Neurgamma."

There was no break in the music that came from the piano or in the soft humming that came from the pianist.

"I can tell you how you took the cultures. But a much more interesting question, doctor, is can you tell me what you've done with them?"

Unlike Kate, Bill didn't raise his gaze from the fire's glow.

"If you tell me I took them, I accept it," he said. "But I have not the faintest idea where they are now."

He half turned towards Kate.

"Maybe I can unlock the memory if I get the right sort of help. The information's there all right. It just needs unscrambling."

"So how do we do that?"

"I've told you what I remember, up to that bizarre meeting

133

in the boardroom. If you tell me what happened after that, I might pick up the thread."

"OK let's try. After that meeting . . ."

She drew an exaggeratedly deep breath.

"Gosh, you don't know how odd this is, telling you about things that you were heavily involved in. Still, after that meeting, the feeling we all had when we first went to the Centre came back, the feeling of starting at a new school. Except that now we felt like new arrivals at a reformatory.

"The meeting, you may remember, was in the evening and, after it, we opened a lot of bottles and all got very angry in the mess. Except for Rex, of course. He kept well out of the way. When we talked, some odd things fell into place. Do you remember, for instance, how they'd run down the staff? We'd been so caught up with the trials we hadn't really noticed.

"Paddy Shaughnessy had found out that all the staff had been confined to barracks for forty-eight hours. They'd been told it was some sort of security exercise and most of them thought it a bit of a lark. Emergency beds for non-residents. Canteen turned into a dormitory. Jolly wartime camaraderie.

"Tim wanted to call a full staff meeting to protest but you bright eyes, pointed out that we couldn't really trust any of them because a fair number would be on the colonel's payroll And, with their help, the colonel could sabotage anything the rest of us decided to do."

"Most of us didn't really catch on to what had happened til we brooded our way into our hangovers early next morning Hangover day was when they started to spell out the nev security rules. Your investigators, for instance, were having to sign the Official Secrets Act and, in future, their results woul go not directly to you but to a new 'data clearance centre'. A would all correspondence about the trials.

"You may remember . . . the question's rhetorical but helps me sit here and tell you things I feel you know . . . yo may remember there are no outside lines at the Centre and a telephone calls have to go through the switchboard. They' probably been monitored all along but that day the monitorir became official.

"The day before, apparently, you'd been talking to one of your investigators and had started talking about delays in publishing results. After a bit, you thought you were getting little response from the other end and found you were talking down a dead line."

Bill shrugged his shoulders. No remnant of memory flickered.

"Under the new rules, all telephone contact with outsiders had to be made by telephonists working in the 'data clearance centre' who would pass on or take messages for us. It seemed a petty bit of bureaucracy. As Greg pointed out, once the forty-eight hours were up anyone who wanted to make a private call could walk down to the village with a handful of ten-pence pieces.

"When those hours were up we discovered why they'd needed them. A lot of soldiers appeared around the place and there were new checks at the gate. Anyone leaving the Centre had to sign out, say where they were going and give the time they expected to be back. And when we left we were searched. Everyone was subjected to a rather degrading body-search and all bags had to be opened. They went through every document line by line and opened any sealed envelopes and read what was inside. Any document they didn't clear had to be left behind.

"When Greg went down to the pub on the first evening, they found some crumpled instructions for a pocket calculator that had been screwed up in his top pocket for so long he couldn't even remember when he'd had the calculator. Yet he still had to leave them at the gatepost and collect them on the way back."

"Next morning Paddy complained to Rex at his departmental meeting that he didn't fancy working under martial law. Rex just laughed and took the line that we'd made the bed and we couldn't complain when we were made to lie on it. So Paddy launched into a noisy tirade about personal freedom and the British constitution, which I'm told sounded like a mixture of Sidney Carton beneath the scaffold and a back-bench MP wishing Godspeed to the Falklands Task Force. But all Rex did was walk out.

"Most of their activity during that forty-eight hours had gone on elsewhere. When the time limit was up you, my love, were the first to leave camp, your pockets a-jingle with ten-pence pieces. When you got back, you joined us in the canteen and you were pretty down in the mouth. You'd been given the cold shoulder by the *Lancet*; the BMA had told you they'd had a meeting with a cabinet minister about the Centre but if you put what you wanted to say in writing it would be carefully considered; and the final blow had come when you got on to that young chum of yours, your ex-student who's just joined the *British Journal of Medicine*, Chris Whatsisname. He told you his editor had been to some top-level meeting and, for the time being, they weren't prepared to print anything about the Centre.

"They'd also been warned off you as an unreliable source. Chip on shoulder. Unsound. Troublemaker. Paranoid. You'd been awarded all the pejorative labels beloved of our medical establishment.

"After that, a sort of communal depression set in. We took to shuffling round in groups except for Greg Wilkinson who kept to himself, spoke to no one unless it was essential, and spent most of the time locked away in his room or his office. For some reason you took against me and became very thick with Tim Craddock. And Sexy Rexy went lording it around the place as though nothing had happened.

"He even called his regular weekly progress meeting. We al turned up and sat around sullenly and Greg told him he wa wasting his time; none of us were doing any work because we' other things on our mind. Rex just smiled one of those nauseating smiles and gave us a little sermon about grown u persons behaving like children, how if we thought through th issues carefully we'd appreciate that our Lords and Masters— God, how I hate that phrase—really had no alternative an were acting in our own best interests, and how he was sure tha next week we'd probably take a different view of things. Th sad thing was that not one of us spoke up. Not even you o Tim. We just listened to him in silence and stared at the tabl until he'd smiled his way out of the room."

Bill produced no response. His attention seemed focused o

the spluttering logs. Marion seemed lost in an evocation of Carroll Gibbons that demanded neither singing nor humming.

"Two nights later we were all woken violently at three in the morning when every fire-alarm in the camp went off. There was a mad panic in the corridors and on the stairways and we ended up milling around on the lawn. Most of us, staff and off-duty Security, were wearing dressing-gowns or raincoats; on-duty Security were dashing around in their uniforms.

"One of the prefabs behind the animal house had gone up and there was Tim Craddock jumping around like a dervish in front of the flames and pointing at the roof of the main house where he'd spotted two men. Then there was a burst of flame from the roof and a couple of dark green fire-engines appeared—odd how that colour made them look as though they weren't real fire-engines so couldn't be any use—and soldiers with hoses sprayed the prefab and climbed up on the roof and sprayed that. Then the colonel appeared in his dressing-gown and told us the excitement was over and we could go back to bed.

"As we walked in, Paddy Shaughnessy came up to me and asked had I seen you. And I hadn't. I didn't tell him I'd tried hard to find you—and, honest, I had—and he assumed you were somewhere in the crowd. Next morning at breakfast, no Bill and no Tim."

Kate paused to take a sip from the brandy glass that stood on the table beside her.

Bill spoke without raising his gaze from the fire.

"This may seem an odd question," he said, "but what was Tim Craddock wearing that night?"

Kate frowned.

"I'll have to work at it. I can remember the silhouette in front of the flames. Track-suit trousers. Sweat shirt. Running shoes, I think."

"The sweat shirt. Anything special about it?"

Kate shrugged.

"Shabby. Dark blue," she said. "Something printed on the front. Nothing saucy."

137

"A tiger's head and three words: 'San Diego Zoo'," said Bill.

"That's it," said Kate. "How odd."

Bill smiled.

"Madam," he said, "I think you've just dialled one of the numbers in the combination lock."

Chapter Fourteen

"Went there on holiday when I was sixteen," said Tim. "Last holiday I had with my parents. I remember the beach and the surfing better than I do the zoo. You said wear something dark and this is the only dark sweater I have."

They looked one another up and down and Bill suffered an attack of nervous giggling which immediately infected Tim. They looked like a pair of inadequate actors in a POW escape film made when Jack Hawkins and Kenneth More were unavailable. Maybe they'd have got away with it in black and white but this was a full-colour real-life production.

Tim was almost acceptable in his jogger's trousers and sweat shirt. He could have passed for a rugby player setting out for an evening's road work, but only if some position on the rugby field could be filled by Aubrey Beardsley. As for Bill, his jeans, black sweater, and black gloves would have been acceptable, as would the smears of mud on his forehead and cheeks, if he hadn't pulled a black woollen tea cosy over his head.

The slightly hysterical jokiness helped suppress the fear which neither wished to acknowledge. A couple of respectable bourgeois dressed up to play adventure games. The analogy with POW films was not far-fetched. Forty and more years before, young middle-class men had been plucked from their Laburnum Avenues and sent off to play heroes. Bill suspected that their war had seemed just as unreal to them, except when the bullets were flying. For the last two hours he'd had the feeling he was on a Field Day with the cadet corps. Any minute the headmaster would ride up on a horse, blow his whistle, and they would form up and march back to school.

Stealing the seed cultures had been ridiculously easy. Bureaucracy, as always, had proved the enemy of security. Seed cultures of the *E coli* that produced Neurgamma in the vats in the Centre's basement were kept in petri dishes, flat glass dishes where the bacteria grew on a jelly-like medium containing the nutrients they needed. The dishes, each coded with a number wax-pencilled on its cover, were kept on racks in a locked annexe to the cold store in the basement. There the temperature was low enough to inhibit their growth without killing them off. At room temperature, the bacteria proliferated and produced the substance that made them precious.

The storeroom that contained them had a double combination lock. The combinations were changed frequently and one was known only to the security section, the other only to research staff authorized to enter the room. One of Tim's jobs was to make regular checks on the cultures and, four days before, he had gone through the familiar routine.

He sought out the duty security man in his office in the basement and they both went to the cold store. The security man dialled his combination, Tim dialled his, and together they pulled the heavy door open. The security man stood in the doorway while Tim walked up and down the racks, picking up an occasional glass dish, taking off the lid, examining the culture within, and making notes on a clipboard before returning the dish to the rack.

When he'd finished, he nodded to the security man who came in and counted the number of plates in each rack, checked that the count tallied with the numbers on *his* clipboard and, when it did, signed it and got Tim to countersign. Then they both swung the heavy door into place and spun the combination dials.

A sound bureaucratic system with a representative of each of two communities, which had been encouraged to see themselves in conflict, checking the activity of the other. Yet it had two flaws. First, though the security man was well briefed on the routine, he had no knowledge of bacteriology second, over the months the security man had come to regard Tim less as an object of suspicion than as an invariably cheerful acquaintance.

No one could therefore blame him for failing to notice what

had actually happened that afternoon. Tim's clipboard had carried not just a sheet of paper but, wedged under the clip, two narrow glass slides with a thin layer of nutrient jelly between them. When Tim was at the end of the room furthest from the security guard he had apparently gone through his usual routine of taking a petri dish from the rack and resting it on his clipboard while he took off the cover, inspected the culture and, before returning the dish to the rack, made a note on his sheet of paper. What he had in truth done, while his hand was hidden from the doorway by the tilted clipboard, was to separate the glass slides and place one for a second, jelly side down, on the culture in the dish. Then, still using the cover provided by the angled board, he had put the slides together again, and placed them under the clip, before he openly put the lid back on the petri dish and returned it to the rack. While he inspected the next dish, he slipped the sheet of paper on his board from under the clip and then clipped it back over the slides to hide them.

The security guard had counted the dishes and found none missing and Tim had countersigned his form. One day an inquisitive person might find the smear he had left across the cultures in one dish but that day could be a long time coming.

Twenty minutes later, Tim and Bill had plated out the specimen that Tim had captured on to eight glass petri dishes which they incubated under a pile of towels in the airing cupboard at the end of their corridor. Twenty-four hours later they knew they had an uncontaminated growth of their quarry in each dish, and the plates were transferred to rest unmarked and anonymous among the assorted specimens which Tim kept in the refrigerator in his office.

On the evening they were dressed as POW escapers, the petri dishes lay on Bill's bed, packed in a special vacuum case devised by the Centre for the transportation of specimens. The temperature inside the case would inhibit bacterial growth for at least seventy-two hours, longer if the dry ice in the outer shell were replaced. From the outside, the case looked like one of the containers elderly gentlemen use to transport their woods to the bowling green.

Beside the case lay two pairs of wire cutters, one with long handles, one with short. They came from the prefab store behind the animal house where they were used to cut the metal bindings from the crates in which supplies arrived. That store was now in disarray, with straw packing and wood shavings from the crates strewn across the floor and sprinkled with every species of inflammable liquid Bill and Tim could find on the shelves.

Bill looked at his watch.

"Best make sure we both have the same time."

He knew that if he said "synchronize our watches" the giggling would restart.

"Five minutes to go," said Tim.

After they'd fiddled with their watches they sat uneasily alongside one another on the edge of the bed.

"Best run through the timings again," said Bill.

So they did. But it didn't fill many of the seconds that were dragging by. The plan was simple, the few essential timings fixed ineradicably in their minds.

Uneasy silence settled once more between them. Then Tim started to speak, at first softly as though speaking to himself and, even when his voice grew louder, he didn't look at Bill but at his knees.

"I know this is going to work," he said, "and I'm glad you've let me be part of it. Sometimes life is so bloody and so unfair that you have to make some sort of gesture to show you don't approve; that this won't do; that you're not part of the mindless mob. Most of the gestures I've made have been pretty fatuous and as emotionally rewarding as a child stamping its foot in frustration. But now I'm actually involved in an act that means something and is likely to achieve something. And for that dear Bill, I will remain eternally grateful."

He raised his head and Bill could see tears glistening on both his cheeks. Then suddenly he turned to Bill and hugged him and Bill hugged him back, and each drew from the other a strength which some people call courage but which, at that moment, Bill knew was nothing more than a resolution to suppress fear. The moment was so deeply imprinted that i

142

would remain in his memory when all around it was washed away.

No more words were spoken. They parted and Bill looked at his watch. The critical second had arrived. He showed the watch to Tim who stood and wiped both cheeks roughly with the back of his forearm. Then he picked up the short-handled wire cutters from the bed and put them in the back pocket of his jeans. He turned and gave Bill a shy smile and was gone.

Bill had to wait for a full six minutes. Tim had gone first to the roof where he would put a match to the fire they had built that afternoon against one of the chimneys: rolls of newspaper, a box of firelighters from the mess cupboard, half a dozen mattresses, and three straw-filled crates. The six minutes dragged but eventually ran out. Bill left his room and walked as softly as he could along the corridors of the mess, dimly lit by a night-light at each end. He climbed out through the ground-floor window that had been used by Tim and headed away from the house across the lawn towards the southernmost section of the floodlit perimeter fence. When he got to the edge of the bright band of light that turned the grass an unreal green for thirty feet each side of the fence, he lay flat on his belly at the very fringe of darkness and facing the fence. The long-handled wire cutters lay alongside him on his right, the case with the cultures on his left.

He wished they'd been able to devise some way to fuse the lights. That was something that came easier in films than in real life. They couldn't even work out where the power came from and Bill was sure that, had they found a way to interrupt the main supply, there would be an emergency back-up. Under the floodlights the tight mesh of the fence seemed fashioned of thicker, tougher wire than he had seen in his casual daylight inspections and, as he lay there staring at it, their plan seemed hopelessly amateurish and fragile.

He looked at his watch. Tim would now be at the storeroom. That shouldn't take long to set ablaze. Bill watched the seconds tick down and then, bang on cue, came the piercing electronic warble of the Centre's fire-alarm. Tim would have relished that moment, fulfilling a fantasy he'd had so often when he passed the notice outside his lab: "In emergency break glass and press button".

Now Tim would be sprinting across the lawn to the northern perimeter. where he hoped he'd have time to cut a few strands of wire in three widely separated places in case Security had some way of instantly detecting the sites of assaults upon their fence. Bill's hope was that, with their men responding to the fire-alarm, they might not have enough reserves to cope immediately with a fourth breach.

He counted off the seconds. One hundred and eighteen . . . one hundred and nineteen . . . one hundred and twenty. Tim would now have run his gamut of diversions. Bill jumped up and raced forward to the wire. The twenty-yard dash helped burn up excess adrenalin but the wire was more difficult than he'd expected. He'd been able to practise only on the metal bands around the crates and some thin wire they'd found in the storeroom. This plastic-covered wire was thick and tough. The first cut took an eternity as he made repeated bites at it and the cutter blades skewed sideways on the plastic. Then he realized he was not using the full leverage of the handles. He moved his hands to the ends of them and, when he did, he sliced through the wire with just one cut.

Behind him he could still hear the warble of the alarm and then added noises. Shouts? The roar of an engine? He didn't look back but concentrated on his cutting. More quickly than he'd hoped he'd made a hole large enough to wriggle through. He threw the cutters away, pushed the case with the cultures through ahead of him and, as he wriggled after it, the back of his sweater caught on a cut end of wire. He kept going and there was a nasty tearing noise.

He dashed down a grassy slope beyond the fence, crossed a metalled road and then forced his way through a bushy hedge that tore at his clothing even more hungrily than had the cut ends of the wire. On the far side of the hedge he paused to draw breath and, as he did, he heard the roar of a Land Rover engine and saw headlights sweeping up the road. He turned and ran across the field beyond the hedge. It was rough pasture and his running shoes gave his ankles little protection as each footstep hit the ground at a different angle. But he didn't slow. He'd have to risk a sprain. Behind him the roar of the Land Rover turned to a rumble. It had come to a halt and the engine was ticking over. Then he heard shouts. Please God they would go to the wire first.

He reached the edge of the woods above the village but before he could enter them he first had to leap the ditch that surrounded the field. As he took off, his right foot slipped and he landed, left foot first, in the bottom of the ditch. His left leg went deep into mud up to mid-calf and he had to drag himself out and up the far side of the ditch.

Once he was in the wood, the going became easier as he trotted across a carpet of pine needles. Navigation was also easy. He just had to move in the opposite direction from the noise behind him. Suddenly the noise changed as someone switched off the fire-alarm. But he could still hear shouting. How close were the shouts? Was he deceiving himself when he decided they were far away? He kept running but allowed himself a glance over his shoulder before he got too deep into the wood. All he saw was darkness. No flames. Maybe Tim had failed as a fire-raiser, but he'd certainly not failed as a causer of commotion.

Having looked, Bill stood still and listened. He heard no sound of pursuers coming across the field after him. Yet they must have found the hole in the fence by now. He was indulging in self-deception. The security guards were trained professionals. They would pursue in silence. He turned and padded on through the wood.

Eventually he reached the lane that ran round the back of the village. As it emerged from the wood, it turned a corner and there beside the bus stop was his first quarry, the phone box.

He entered it and rested his back gratefully against the side glass. He dug out the handful of ten-pence pieces Tim and he had collected and placed them in a neat pile on top of the coin box. Then he raised the receiver, pushed five of the coins into the slot, and tapped out the number.

As he tapped, he screwed his eyes tight trying to decipher the number on each button. Damned difficult. They were more like buttons on a pocket calculator than on a telephone. If the phone had had a dial he might have remembered the movement of his finger but here there were only buttons and, try as he might, he couldn't see the numbers. And now they melted to a glowing red beneath the logs, and Marion was playing, and Kate was staring at him anxiously, and he couldn't remember the bloody number that he'd dialled.

Chapter Fifteen

Kate was silent, a straight-backed figure at the edge of his vision. She had delivered the last of her slow and deliberate cross-questions. Each had been one Bill had posed himself during the desperate seconds he'd tried to remember the number. And when Kate asked the questions, the answers stayed unchanged.

No, he hadn't rung the *Lancet*. Nor the BMA, nor a newspaper. He didn't want another rebuff. They'd probably have had as little time for him with the cultures as they'd had for him without. Even worse, they might betray him.

And no, he hadn't rung a solicitor. Tim and he had argued the possibilities over and over and they'd made a clear decision. That he did remember. After what had happened since the clampdown, they decided they would trust nobody. Before approaching anyone, they would hide the seed cultures and only Bill would know where they were.

With the cultures safely hidden, they could bargain. They would offer to hand them back if the MOD took the wraps off the Centre and let everyone know what they had achieved. And if the MOD hesitated, they would point out that some of the journalists who had fobbed them off might pay more attention when they produced the evidence. They wouldn't go to the press, unless forced to. They just wanted the MOD to come clean. The cultures were their bargaining counter and, as long as they remained hidden, neither Tim nor Bill could be betrayed.

"And where were you to be while all this bargaining went on?"

"You've now reached the point," said Bill, "where I can answer only with a riddle."

"Try me," said Kate.

"I was to go into hiding . . ." He pulled a long face and

raised both shoulders in exaggerated apology. ". . . I was to go into hiding with a fox."

Kate stared at him. Then her stare melted to a smile.

"You're offering a metaphor? A lair? Going to ground?"

"Don't tell the psychiatrists but the only image my memory digs out is that of the red-coated animal hunted by men in even redder coats."

Kate's quizzical smile remained unchanged.

"Then a red-coated fox it has to be, Brother Reynard."

She had turned her head away, and again she sat still and silent, her face lit by the glow of the fire, her spiky urchin hair darkened by shadow. Bill could sense her wanting to move close to him. Or could he? Self-pity was a close cousin to self-deception. What he needed now was not self-pity but anger. Yet each day anger seemed to come less readily, as if during the past weeks he had overdrawn on his reserves.

He turned towards Kate and tried a grin. He was never sure what was meant by a hangdog expression but he suspected if he'd looked in a mirror at that moment he would have seen one.

Kate came out of her reverie.

"Tim did a better job than you thought," she said. "Security's first guess was that intruders had broken in through the holes he'd cut at the top end of the park; broken in, started the fires, and then got out. The pathetic little hole you cut was written off as a diversion."

Bill summoned up a lukewarm smile. A hangdog smile?

"Eventually they shepherded us all back to the mess but most of us hung out of our windows gossiping and trying to find out what was going on. From where we were it looked as though they were concentrating their search at the north end of the park and those woods beyond. I suspect the men in the Land Rover you saw just checked the hole in the wire, reported on their radio, and drove off to join the others."

"So I could have walked," said Bill. "And I needn't have rushed that ditch. I could smell the mud I landed in for days."

"Hang on," said Kate. "For how many days?"

Bill looked at her blankly.

"For how many days? And where were you?"